*A World Apart*

# A WORLD APART

Shawn Slovo

*faber and faber*

LONDON · BOSTON

First published in 1988
by Faber and Faber Limited
3 Queen Square London WCIN 3AU

Photoset by Wilmaset Birkenhead Wirral
Printed in Great Britain by
Richard Clay Ltd Bungay Suffolk

*British Library Cataloguing in Publication Data*

Slovo, Shawn
A world apart.
I. Title
822'.914   PR6069.L5/
ISBN 0–571–15235–X

# Contents

*Chris Menges and Shawn Slovo*

# Introduction

I was born in South Africa. I lived there for the first thirteen years of my life, until 1964. In 1963, three years after the Sharpeville massacre and the first State of Emergency, my father, Joe Slovo, was forced underground and then, following the Rivonia Trial, into exile. My mother, Ruth First, was the first white woman to be detained under the Ninety-Day Detention Act. After her release, after 117 days in solitary confinement, the family – my mother, her parents, myself and my two younger sisters – joined my father in exile in London.

*A World Apart* takes place in South Africa in 1963. It focuses on the relationship between a white woman, politically committed to the fight against apartheid, and her thirteen-year-old daughter, who must contend against politics for the love, care and time of her mother. Set against a backdrop of increasingly violent repression, it chronicles the effects of the break-up of the family. Above all, it's about the child's attempts to come to terms with the political choices her parents have made.

I've worked in the film industry since 1974, as a secretary, researcher, story editor. In 1978 I relocated to New York because I thought you had to be over there, where the money and the audiences are, and where most of the films are made. I worked for Robert De Niro on *Raging Bull* and *The King of Comedy*. The privilege of working that close with such major talent aside, I became an expert in downtown loft conversions, beach-house maintenance and organic foods shopping. I spent most of my working time on the telephone, and with Ivy in the 'At Your Service' department of Bloomingdale's.

In 1978, my mother had settled in Mozambique, as the Director of Research at the Centre for African Studies at the University of Eduardo Mondlane in Maputo. On 17 August 1982, she was assassinated by a parcel bomb in her office at the university. The phone call with the news of her death was one that I'd been expecting for most of my life. I had always imagined it would be about my father. The only white member of the National Executive of the African National Congress, his had always been the high profile: 'Public Enemy No. 1', 'Teddybear Terrorist',

'Revolutionary Pimpernel', 'the KGB Colonel with a dacha outside Moscow', as he is described by the South African press. It's a phone call I still expect today. The white nationalist regime in South Africa is intent on maintaining itself and perpetuating its power, and its stated purpose is to liquidate members of the main democratic movement, the ANC, both in exile and in the country.

The last time I spoke to my mother on the telephone, we had an argument. The day before her death I received a letter from her; one to her from me was *en route* to Mozambique. For most of my adult life, ours had been an intense, interrupted and volatile relationship. I'd visited her in Maputo the year before, and she'd spent ten days with me in New York in April 1982. For the first time – and this is something we both felt – we were each making efforts to stabilize the relationship, to confront and talk about the past, about the anger, about the guilt.

After her funeral in Maputo, I returned to England and in 1983 enrolled as a writing student at the National Film and TV School. Almost immediately I began to write the screenplay that turned into *A World Apart*. It didn't matter what writing assignment was set us, I kept writing around and about the subject of my relationship with my mother, in the context of the national liberation struggle in South Africa. I chose to set the story in the past, and to tell it through the eyes of a thirteen-year-old, because I calculated that it would be more accessible for others, western audiences in particular. My mother's own account of her period in solitary confinement in 1963, *117 Days*, was by my side, though it was a long time before I could bring myself to reread it. After her release, and in her own words in the last sentence in the book, 'When they left me in my own house at last I was convinced that it was not the end, that they would come for me again.'

I knew I had to write it small, in terms of the budget, simply because that was its only chance of being made. I had to work out ways to explain the political background to potential audiences who would know nothing about the system of apartheid, and how to merge the politics with the personal, without detracting from the importance of either.

For most of the next two years I struggled to turn what was a confused, unresolved and highly personal story into something that would touch others. I owe a lot to Colin Young and the support structure at the National Film School. When my father was in town, his input proved invaluable. I formed my own writer's group of Gillian Slovo, Andy Metcalf and Clare Downs who kept me on course in their collective scrutiny of each draft of the screenplay.

In the early drafts there was a cloying self-pity and a stubborn anger: the thirteen-year-old too much the passive victim, the white racist characters caricatured and stereotyped, the grandmother more of a villain than the villains. Most of all, I battled with the relationship between the mother and daughter, particularly with the final scene between the two of them, when the daughter confronts her mother with her attempted suicide bid in prison. 'You tried to leave us. You don't care about us. You shouldn't have had us.' In life, that was what kept us apart. In life, that was the conversation, the confrontation, my mother and I had never had.

In February 1986, I took it out into the world. I flirted for a while with America: Jane Fonda Incorporated had a problem with the fact that there were two major South African projects in development and felt they would be starting a race they had little chance of finishing. Another company didn't want to do a period piece. In their opinion there would be greater emotional impact with something contemporary. This was a constant criticism: what's the relevance of setting a story about South Africa in the past, wouldn't a contemporary piece be more relevant and interesting for audiences, isn't there a danger that the film will be out of date, and if it's set in the past, why isn't it openly autobiographical, in which case the date is part of its authenticity. From that kind of feedback, it was as if I had written the 'wrong' script.

Because South Africa is a topical subject, and because *A World Apart* could be made relatively cheaply, there was a certain amount of interest among British producers. I agonized over which producer – not so much because there was any real competition in the end, but because I had a great deal of difficulty letting it go. My agent, Jenne Casarotto, introduced me to Sarah Radclyffe and Working Title, the company she set up with Tim Bevan. Sarah has commitment, warmth, humour and inexhaustible supplies of energy. She helped to pinpoint the story changes that had to be made, woke up with the crew during shooting, and sat with Chris Menges and Nic Gaster, the editor, during cutting. Working Title as a company functions in an unusually non-oligarchic and – for this country – dynamic way. They fly economy, like everyone else, and the money goes on the film.

Chris Menges had been sent the screenplay in his role as Director of Photography. His response was that he'd like to direct it. This would be a début for him in feature films, but there wasn't much debate. In his distinguished and varied career, he has never fought shy of head-on confrontation with pressing social and political issues. The very first documentary he worked on, an instalment for *World in Action*, was an exploration of the conflicts that have torn South Africa apart. This was in Johannesburg, in 1963, the setting and the time of the story of *A World Apart*. He's an (annoyingly) self-effacing, modest and gentle man, with a laser-sharp vision and an intense political focus and integrity. He has no problems working with women, and he's not afraid to say what he doesn't know. He inspires enormous loyalty and respect, and it is this factor that is, in large part, responsible for the high calibre of the production – especially in respect to the technical crew: the best of the British can pick and choose what they do. Bulawayo in Zimbabwe can't exactly be described as an exotic location and they certainly couldn't have been doing it for the money.

Sarah and Chris committed themselves to the project in June 1986. Sarah started to raise the money and went to Worthing to make *Wish You Were Here*. Chris went to Louisiana to light *Shy People*. I stayed at home and worried and rewrote and worried. In January 1987, we flew to Zimbabwe for the first recce, then again in March for the definitive recce. Back in England, I rewrote and worried and rewrote as they crewed and cast the film. On 15 June 1987, the cameras rolled in downtown Bulawayo on the first day of principal photography.

## Extracts from a Diary – 1987

1 JANUARY
You can't make a film in Zimbabwe without approval from the
Ministry of Information. We've sent them the script and the
proposed schedule and we get a letter back giving us the go-ahead.

8 JANUARY
Sarah, Caroline Hewitt (the Production Manager) and I lie around
the blob-shaped puddle, a poor excuse for a swimming pool, on the
roof of Miekeles Hotel in downtown Harare, sipping sickly sweet,
green sugar-rimmed tumblers of Malawi shandies, recovering
from the overnight flight from London. We're a little lost: this trip
is a first for all of us and we've no idea whether Zimbabwe can
stand in for the South Africa of the script. Richard Attenborough's
just done it, with *Cry Freedom*, but he had all the resources in the
world. We can't afford to build – we have to make do with what we
see.

9 JANUARY
A meeting with the Film Officer, Beverly Tilley, at the Ministry of
Information. She's surprised to see us. She had submitted our
script to the Minister and because it's set in South Africa and its
politics are the politics of the African National Congress, we need
script approval from the ANC before we can be given the go-ahead
by Zimbabwe. Beverly had been away and had left two letters with
her secretary, pending the Minister's decision. One said yes, the
other yes but. The wrong one had been sent out to us. The
Department of Information of the ANC is based at its headquarters in Lusaka, Zambia. Back at the hotel, I start the long and
impossible task of trying to find out whether my father is in
Lusaka.

10 JANUARY
We switch hotels to the Sheraton, where the telephones work. I
finally manage to locate Joe. I explain our problem. He's emphatic: this is not his department and he has never pulled rank before
and is certainly not going to start on behalf of one of his daughters.

I tell him I'll be flying to Lusaka tomorrow. He says it will be nice to see me, but he's busy so someone else will meet me.

## 14 JANUARY

I arrive in Lusaka without a yellow fever inoculation. Joe meets me at the airport and manages to convince the authorities not to send me back.

## 15 JANUARY

I step off the Lusaka to Harare flight, waving a piece of paper. The script has been approved by the Department of Information of the ANC. We hand-deliver the letter to Beverly Tilley.

We're on a weekend and rack our brains to try and justify a location recce to Victoria Falls. We go anyway. In the walk through the rain forest we get a chance to try out our safari gear. We giggle at the Japanese tourists wearing shower caps and raincoats, until my brand-new sun hat bleeds blue dye all over my pristine whites. Sarah and Caroline discover that pith helmets, though they look great, are unbearably hot and heavy.

## 19 JANUARY

We get the go-ahead from the Minister. Sarah and Caroline swing into action, meeting potential Zimbabwean crew. The country's facilities are, for the most part, geared to hosting foreign-based crews and there's a solid base of experience to draw from, thanks to the productions of Philip Saville's *Mandela*, and *Cry Freedom* and Cannon (*Sheena – Queen of the Jungle*) before that. The problems of filming in a third-world country – lack of processing and lab facilities, shortages of equipment, shortcomings in transport provisions – are thoroughly researched and anticipated. Caroline spends most of her time negotiating the catering franchise. Our crew will be for the most part British and she doesn't want to give them the lever of unsatisfactory food. Sarah tells her not to bother – they'll complain anyway.

I sit in on some of the meetings, to avoid getting too far ahead in the suntan stakes.

## 20 JANUARY

Chris flies in. He's nervous, and so are we: we're all still getting to know each other. He's anxious to get to Bulawayo. He's recced both cities recently for a Warner Bros André Brink project, *A Dry White Season*. He's pretty certain that Bulawayo can be more easily adapted to resemble and represent Johannesburg in 1963, or at least those parts of the city in which the story takes place. He also knows that logistically it's going to be easier to make the film in the smaller, less cosmopolitan, neglected southern capital.

21 JANUARY
We fly to Bulawayo, escorted by our Zimbabwean Location Manager, Rory Kilalea. We check into the Holiday Inn, with whom we've negotiated a deal, on the basis of future business. As usual, Chris, the foreign man of the party, gets the executive suite, a bowl of fruit and a key to the mini-bar. They don't understand it's Sarah, the keeper of the purse, they should be flattering. She couldn't give a damn.

At a first glance, and in many ways, it's immediately apparent that Bulawayo is more suited than Harare to our needs. Inner-city construction in the last thirty years has been minimal; the outlying plush white suburbs, the legacy of colonial rule, can easily substitute for their counterparts in South Africa; twenty-year-old action vehicles are more the rule than the exception.

24 JANUARY
Crammed in a rented Peugeot, we've spent the past four days in the white suburbs, searching for the main Roth house location (modest) and a house for the Abelson family (flamboyant). Rory wakes at five in the morning to prepare the groundwork – by lunchtime he's exhausted. He tells us how on *Cry Freedom* they built Donald Woods's house. Sarah tells him to forget about it.

Chris wants to see every single suburban house, and it's 35° Centigrade. He's constantly taking me aside: is this like your garden, is this like your kitchen, is this like your corridor. The problem is I don't remember all that well.

To avoid antagonizing or alienating potential possibilities, Rory becomes adept at minimalizing the political content of the film, describing it in a mumble as a 'mother–daughter' story. I'm never introduced in full – Slovo is an inflammatory name in these parts. These are white Zimbabweans who still call themselves Rhodesians. They complain all the time: about the servants, the

3

shortages, the foreign currency regulations and the integration of schools. They seriously expect our sympathy.

We unwind at sunset in the Matopas National Park. We can understand why Cecil Rhodes left instructions to be buried there, though there can't have been much left of him after the slow trek up from Cape Town.

Caroline spends a lot of time in the kitchens, negotiating the food. The hotel promises to introduce new menus.

25 JANUARY
We've a shortlist for the Roth house location. Extensive recces of the high-density housing areas on the outskirts of the city. It's clear that, with careful and creative adaptation, the scenes in the script set in the township of Soweto could be located here. We'll never be able to show that much because we don't have that kind of budget. Or for mass crowd scenes – Chris wants a minimum of 6000 for the final scene in the film, the burial of Solomon. Rory tells us that Richard Attenborough had 22,000 extras for his burial scene. Sarah tells Chris he'll be lucky to get two.

Chris gives Sarah advance warning that he wants a helicopter. We search in vain for its appearance in the script.

Chris is agitating for a real prison for the scenes of Diana's internment – for authenticity – and he's adamant. Beverly Tilley is not encouraging, for obvious reasons of security. Chris won't let go and the relevant Ministry is approached for permission to film inside one of the prisons. Sarah quietly apportions part of the budget for the construction of a prison.

A decision is made to commence principal photography on 15 June, to coincide with the dry season for continuity of weather. We'll miss the jacaranda season, when the suburbs are transformed by a mass of purple blossom, just like Johannesburg, and it hasn't properly rained in Bulawayo for years, but with our budget we can't take any chances. I write out one of the two scenes requiring rain in the script. The second one's at night, and we can fake it.

FEBRUARY 1987
Back to London. Sarah, with Tim Bevan and Graham Bradstreet, the financial controller and third partner of Working Title, raises the money.

The casting director, Susie Figgis, begins the herculean task of finding the thirteen-year-old to play the daughter, Molly. This is our biggest nightmare: if she doesn't work out then neither will the film. The story is for the most part her point of view and if she can't carry the narrative then we might as well go home. And this is something we'll never be sure of until we start filming.

I retreat to rewrite. I'm reworking and strengthening the dialogue, tightening the structure, reworking some of the characters, particularly the still-stereotyped villains of the piece. As far as Chris is concerned, and it's one of the things that he brings to the script, he wants it opened out wherever possible to show apartheid in action. He wants the audience to see as much as possible of the world in which the drama takes place. I'm not only restricted by the limits of the budget, but also by the point of view. There's a limit to how many situations showing the brutalities of apartheid a thirteen-year-old white middle-class child would witness, without standing accused of convenience. Even in our family we were protected. I'm zealously guarding Molly's point of view as the focus for the audience because when we lose that, the delicate balance of the whole is undermined. Also, the script has been timed, and it's twenty minutes too long. That amount of cutting involves a lot more than topping and tailing.

In the pattern of the past two years, I avoid writing the Final Confrontation scene between the mother and daughter. It's the resolution – in so far as this issue can be resolved – of the film. There's no proper ending without it. There's no getting around it: all my critics have been united in stressing its importance. And I can't see how I'm going to pull it off.

I battle with rhetoric to write Solomon's call-to-action speech in the church, and the priest's speech at the graveside at the end. My sister Gillian comes through with the basis of the words for the priest, and Solomon's speech goes in the pending file, along with the Final Confrontation.

A second recce looming. I'm paranoid for a few days that I won't be taken along. I'm waiting, and based on what I've consistently witnessed at first hand, for the writer to be rejected.

11 MARCH
Back to Zimbabwe for the definitive recce. All members of the advance party present, accompanied by Brian Morris (Production

Designer), Peter Biziou (Lighting Cameraman). Nic Ede (Costume Designer) and Susie Figgis.

15 MARCH
While Sarah and Caroline deal with the business of film-making, Chris and I hole up for three days in his air-conditioned suite, working on the script. I write in the helicopter. We argue about a train sequence because I feel it takes us right away from the main narrative. That's why he wants it. The scene goes in. It's a low, nervy point for each of us: we're both débuting – he as director, me as writer – and we're too far to turn back. Barney Simon, the South African playwright-director, flies up from Johannesburg for a visit. We read through the script with him, pinpointing the areas that still need work. At the end of the session, the script's still too long. Chris is wondering when I'm going to write Solomon's speech.

17 MARCH
Back to Bulawayo. More recces, though these are, for the most part, technical and don't involve me. Our shortlist of Roth house locations are visited and re-visited. We finally select a house belonging to a Dutch doctor and his family, and they plan a trip to Holland and house improvements they'll be able to make with the fee. At the last minute, while on a solitary sortie, Brian finds a better house, both creatively and technically. The owners are reluctant – even here they've heard the stories about film companies in action. Rory begins the long task of negotiation to change their minds.

20 MARCH
We scour the schools for the exclusive all-white establishment Molly attends in the script. They're now, in theory anyway, all integrated. We're going to have to people it with white girls from every school, to make up the numbers we need. The irony's not lost on us.

21 MARCH
Chris and Susie fly to Johannesburg for the day, to look for actors to play Solomon and Elsie. They're traumatized by the experience. The last time Chris was in Johannesburg he was arrested for taking

photographs of John Vorster Square – which is hardly surprising as that's police headquarters. They use the Market Theatre as a casting base. Most, and many of the best actors are members of the PAC. A black breakaway group since 1959, the PAC takes issue with a major clause in the ANC Freedom Charter which states that 'South Africa belongs to all who live in it, black and white.' They won't have anything to do with a project informed by ANC politics and that centres around white activists. In spite of this resistance Chris finds a Solomon in the end, Albee Lesotho.

23 MARCH

Albee flies up to Harare for a couple of days. He's recently spent eighteen months in prison, and maintains he's not afraid to take this on board. He has a family, and Chris warns him that the filming will mean he'll be separated from them for the best part of three months. Albee looks at Chris as if he's crazy: because of apartheid he can hardly manage to see his children once every six months . . . I go through the script with him. He's wondering about Solomon's speech, and I fantasize for a time that he should write it. We go over what should be included: a brief history of the people's struggle, western investment and complicity, the background to the tactic of armed struggle.

24 MARCH

Susie and Chris have by now seen every single white twelve to fourteen-year-old girl in Zimbabwe. It would be ideal if we can find her here – she'd have the accent and would be familiar with the social context of southern Africa. It doesn't look hopeful, though they find the younger sisters without much difficulty.

Susie and her assistant, Andrew Whaley, tour the local rugby clubs, searching for extras for the military and police presence required by the script. With their memories of the recent war in Zimbabwe, they're defensive and suspicious. They're mostly frightened they and their families will be victimized by the South African authorities if they agree to participate in the film.

28 MARCH

Back to London. We continue the long, drawn-out debate over the title. A search has cleared it for our use, but Chris hates it. He thinks it's difficult to remember, easy to get wrong, and that its

7

meaning's only clear if you've seen the film. Atlantic, the company who've come on board as the American distributor, fax us a list of 72 alternative titles. They include 'Molly's Age' and 'The Age of Molly', 'A Song for Molly' and 'Molly's Song', 'Go Alone' and 'A Long Walk Together', 'Beyond Reason' and 'Beyond Treason', 'The Angry Land' and 'A Land of Anger', 'Dangerous Reason' and 'Unreasonable Danger', 'United in Love' and 'United We Stand'. Our favourite is 'Beat the Golden Bird'.

15 APRIL
They're busy at Working Title, with the final casting and crewing up. I'm not involved, but they keep me posted. I'm still struggling with Solomon's speech, researching the archives of International Defence and Aid, and avoiding the Final Confrontation. In a memorable session at Sarah's flat, with the script spread out across her living room floor, she, Chris and I cut ten minutes. I lose a favourite sequence. When I go back to compare what we have with the early drafts, there's very little that remains in its original form. In the process of rewriting I've panicked over and mourned almost everything I lose. But what's become clearer, and revelatory, is that it's usually an improvement on the whole.

Chris wants incidental dialogue: conversations for the extras at the Roth and Abelson parties, schoolgirls' chatter in the corridors, slogans for the bus boycott. I start eavesdropping all over the place, but I think it's a daft and time-consuming prospect to give extras lines.

24 APRIL
Barbara Hershey, who's to play the mother, Diana, arrives *en route* to the Cannes Film Festival, where she subsequently picked up an award for *Shy People*. As Atlantic Entertainment have invested in a proportion of the budget (the balance is from British Screen and local Zimbabwean finance Graham Bradstreet has raised) it's a foregone conclusion that the actress who plays Diana will be an American and a box-office draw. In our favour, we know that we have an interesting, non-stereotyped and unusual role on offer and that, subject to availability, we'll get someone we know is right. Because this is a low-budget film, she will have to take a not insubstantial drop in salary. This has never been an overriding factor for anyone we've approached.

8

## 26 APRIL

A weekend with Barbara and Chris, meeting South African exiles who are contemporaries of my parents, and longtime friends of the family. These are difficult and often painful sessions for me. It's not that anybody's not sensitive – quite the contrary – but more that, by necessity, there's a briskness and arbitrary selectiveness about the process. The thin line between the private and the public is constantly broached. It must be as hard for Barbara, playing my mother. In the concentration and intensity of these sessions I learn a lot I didn't know, hear things I haven't heard before.

We talk in depth about the nature of my parents' commitment to the national liberation struggle in South Africa. It wasn't so much out of a sense of guilt, out of feelings of being privileged, more because of a profound sense of justice.

A long debate about why we're not using the real names in the script. I was attempting a piece of drama, and I needed the distance from my characters, and the absence of the discomfort I felt when I identified them as members of my family. I did not want to presume to speak for them. And it felt wrong because all the other characters in the screenplay are composite, and the way things actually happened are not always the way they happen in the film. (I named the mother after Princess Diana – I figured I needed all the help I could get to make a woman who was a Communist sympathetic to western audiences . . .)

We talk about the Final Confrontation. We agree on its importance, and that it's sketchy as it is. Barbara feels strongly that there's a problem with the prison scenes in the middle section of the script. There's not enough to show Diana's deterioration to the point where she attempts suicide. We're now at least ten minutes over length, and I don't see where I can fit more words.

## 27 APRIL

Barbara works with the shortlist of Mollys. There's no doubt for her that it's Jodhi May, a twelve-year-old from North London, who was seen by Susie and Chris in the very first batch. I meet Jodhi, but I'm too frightened to communicate much with her.

## 15 MAY

Yvonne Bryceland has agreed to play Bertha, the grandmother.

David Suchet, Paul Freeman and Adrian Dunbar have been cast as the members of the security force. Tim Roth is cast as Harold, and I'm shocked when I meet him because I had written Harold as an unorganized and rather messy activist, a contemporary of Gus's and Diana's. Tim is cool and dapper, and looks at least ten years younger than Diana. Chris tells me to have faith, but I'm not convinced he's not going to be perceived as Diana's toyboy. We're having trouble finding an Elsie. There's no question, though, that she has to be a Southern African.

20 MAY

I've been through the family archives, transcribing letters I think will be of use to the actors. I write character biographies of the family. I've a draft of Solomon's speech, culled from calls to action I've researched. It's ten minutes long, not all that well structured, and bogged down in polemic.

25 MAY

I'm summoned to the Working Title offices by Sarah – something's come up that she can't discuss over the phone. Here it is, I panic, the rejection of the writer. Chris has decided he'll be better off without me. It had to come, it was only a matter of time, it's a foregone conclusion for script-writers, it happened to Faulkner, Fitzgerald, to William Goldman . . .

There's been a panic from Zimbabwe. Because of their proximity to South Africa, and because of recent attacks on members of the ANC, they're concerned that Joe Slovo's daughter will attract attention. If I'm there for the shooting, they can't and won't guarantee the safety of the crew.

28 MAY

We've negotiated a compromise solution, the day before I'm due to fly out. I'll dye my hair, change my name, and check into a different hotel from everyone else. By this point, I'm completely passive. Clarissa Troop, the assistant accountant, renames me Kate Robbins. The hairdresser looks aghast when I tell him I want to go blonde. It won't work for you, he says, and it's not true they have all the fun. We compromise, and I go half-blonde. Five hours later, I'm a furious and frazzled version of myself.

## 30 MAY

Bulawayo. I check in to the Holiday Inn. Now that I'm here, there's no way I'll be separated from the activity. I register as Kate Robbins which confuses the staff who know me as me from the two previous recces.

Chris has memo'd Sarah that he wants a large black tame crow. Sarah's memo'd Chris and me that the script is now eleven minutes and ten seconds overlong. Chris memos me about Solomon's speech, and the Final Confrontation. I haven't yet been allocated an office – they're casting in the room I thought would be mine. There's a typewriter though, only no ribbon cartridges. The secretary at the hotel shows me how to rewind the cartridges, to re-use the ribbon. It's the Zimbabwean way. I think back over the years and all those discarded cartridges.

## 31 MAY

Sarah assembles the crew for a briefing. Because of the politics of the film, there are plain-clothes Zimbabwean CIO security men planted amongst us. She doesn't know who they are, and she doesn't even know who knows who they are. She explains about my change of name – most of the crew have never met me anyway. It's easy for them to call me Kate, harder for me to know they're talking to me. Mark and Mark, the propsman and set decorator, call me Molly.

Rory hands out 'Welcome to Bulawayo' kits. Included is the information that there's not a single restaurant open in the city on Sundays. Also a warning to ensure that all clothing is ironed because the putsi fly lays its eggs in damp clothing.

Supper with Jodhi. The first time we've sat down together. We agree to make it a weekly feature. She looks pale and hunched, a world apart from a child of the southern hemisphere. There's been a rash of memos from Chris urging her to lie in the sun and swim in the pool. Only it's winter. During the week, she's going to a local girls' school, to pick up the accent. She hates it – it's a long way from Camden School for girls.

## 1 JUNE

The long queues for the relatively few jobs, in a country racked by unemployment, begin to form: outside the hotel base, then stretching down the road outside the downtown production offices. The 'No Work' sign makes no difference: these are lines that never abate through to the last day of principal photography. They're coming from all over the country in the hope of work, from Gweru, 200 kilometres to the north, even from Harare, on the overnight train.

A marathon unpacking in Wardrobe – all the period clothing has been shipped over from England. Opposite they're busy casting. Jeremy Brickhill, who was active in Zimbabwe's own liberation struggle, and who has long been associated with anti-apartheid organizations, is employed to help. He knows everybody. Chris wants as many of the actors for the subsidiary parts, both black and white, to be cast from those who, through their personal involvement and direct experience, are familiar with and sympathetic to the people's liberation struggle in southern Africa. Many are South African exiles who have experienced detention and been subjected to torture. Phyllis Naidoo is recruited to pay Saeeda. She was herself detained and then, in exile, the victim of a parcel bomb attack. Joyce Sikakane, one of the film's technical advisers, is a South African exile who spent fourteen months in solitary confinement. Other white and non-white roles are cast from the ranks of Zimbabweans who, because of the recent war of independence here, had similar experiences. These are the people Chris implicitly trusts to give the performances he wants for this story.

2 JUNE

Barbara and I get together to work. She stresses again that there's not enough in the script to show Diana's deterioration to the point where she attempts suicide. She's rewritten most of the prison interrogation scenes, adding and embellishing. The dialogue is taken from the interrogation scenes in Ruth's book, *117 Days*. On the one hand, I feel I'm the protector of Molly's point of view in the script and I know that these extra words are going to play hell with the shooting schedule. And I'm not convinced they're all necessary. On the other hand, Barbara is a serious, experienced, skilled and intelligent actress: if she says she needs more, then who am I to argue with that. She wonders what's happening to the Final Confrontation.

4 JUNE

I finally get an office, and battle with Diana's scenes in the script, trying to add more without adding more. My fear is that the extra words take away from or dilute the narrative thrust of the scene.

7 JUNE
I put the prison stuff aside to struggle with the Final Confrontation. A view on to the hotel gardens, where Jodhi and Nadine (who plays Molly's friend, Yvonne) are learning to twist, hula-hoop and play the castanets. For the best friends they play in the story, they're very suspicious of each other. There's a certain amount of envy involved: every single white thirteen-year-old in Zimbabwe, Nadine included, was once a potential Molly. Jodhi is nervous about what's coming up, and a location film set is not a healthy environment for children to be, never mind to relate to each other.

9 JUNE
I go through the script with Joyce, for a final check on authenticity of detail. In the bus boycott sequence, Diana is dictating into a tape-recorder, describing the scene. Among what she sees are 'mothers, babies tied securely to their backs'. Joyce says there is no way that mothers would take small children with them to work in the white suburbs. They're left at home in the townships, to be looked after by old people or siblings. This is one of the features of apartheid. For me, black domestic workers with their children on their backs are one of my childhood memories. Also, the phrase is taken directly from a report my mother filed on the 1956 bus boycott. We argue back and forth, then put it on ice for the time being.

Chris sends an advance memo asking for butterflies for the school history-lesson scene. I try and argue him out of the scene: I've always hated it. Chris needs it – it's one of the few scenes that shows the ignorance amongst the backbone of South African whites, specifically the distortion of history. He urges me to find a different way to write it. He'll still want butterflies though.

10 JUNE
Improvisation session all day, for the large military and police presence required in the script. Jeremy in charge, his main objective to ensure that those picked will know when to stop when they're actually *in situ* and provoked. One man gets so carried

away, screaming the classic if improvised line 'I'll kill you, you commie bastard' that the hotel staff call in the police, convinced the film company are under attack. Another yanks a phone out of the wall and hurls it across the room, narrowly missing Ms Figgis.

Cont Mhlanga and Simon Shumba, the black crowd coordinators, get to work casting in the high-density housing areas. Cont is a theatre director and is briefed to begin rehearsals for the foreground action in the various crowd scenes.

We finally find our Elsie. She's Linda Mvusi, a South African exile now living in Harare. She's ambivalent about her involvement. I ask her to be critical about the script, particularly the black subplots.

12 JUNE
Albee (Solomon) due to fly in today from Johannesburg. He's not on the plane. Panic in production as we imagine the worst.

Chris is worried about the scene we're scheduled to shoot first thing on the first day. It's the first scene and it's too quiet for an opening, he says. I try to convince him and myself that it's filled with tension. We drive to the location where the construction crew are fighting the deadline and rework it.

Chris gets a response on the butterflies from Lloyd Searle, the Assistant Props buyer. It's illegal to trap butterflies in Zimbabwe, because so many species are protected. Arrangements have been made through the National History Museum that require that we transport 'one entomologist, Philip Mhlanga, with ten traps and rotting fruit with three assistants which we must supply, to and from the Matopas National Park, from Monday to Sunday. The traps will remain *in situ* in the park and will take a day to set up and then have to be cleared every a.m. and p.m. The insects will be transported in closed vehicles to the National History Museum where a controlled environment is being created for them.' Even Chris is speechless.

13/14 JUNE
The last weekend before the first day of principal photography.

Location recces, wardrobe fittings, haircuts, choir practice, meetings, stills and dialect sessions, Spanish dance rehearsals, crowd auditions, police training and police dog-handling courses

14

all weekend. For the few not involved, the options are horse riding and tennis. For reasons of security we're forbidden to drive further than the well-policed thirty kilometres to the Matopas.

Chris and I meet with Barbara to go over the prison scenes. I've now rewritten Barbara's rewrites which has mainly involved cutting back. In the end, we're back to where we started – most of the cuts go back in. Sarah has a scheduling fit. Chris and Barbara wondering about the Final Confrontation . . .

Chris and I revisit the Roth house location. We shift a few props around. After that, a rehearsal with Lovemore and his band who will play at the Roth party scene, with a break for lunch. The pennywhistle-player (a last-minute find on the streets of Bulawayo) is two and a half hours late back and is in no state to play. An executive decision is made that in future he'll be given lunch, not lunch money.

Chris memos the entire unit to feel free to use his suite to view the documentary and archival footage on the period and the politics he's amassed. Most of them are at the race track all day, expanding their per diems.

15 JUNE
The first day of principal photography. I'm on set, not feeling all that comfortable about being there. We ease into shooting with some mute set-ups: Molly waking, getting out of bed, staring out of windows, walking down corridors. Then the first dialogue sequence: the opening scene where Gus (Jeroen Krabbe) says goodbye to Molly, never to reappear again in the story. I'm appalled when Gus, in reply to Molly's probing, answers 'You know I can't talk about it. It's my other work.' Other work? It makes no sense. After a take or two, we cut it. I feel more comfortable about being on set.

Albee's on the plane from Johannesburg. He's yawning and distracted, and surprised at our concern – there was only a confusion on dates. He wants to see Solomon's speech.

16 JUNE
Yvonne Bryceland, who plays the grandmother, Bertha, has a problem with a scene to be shot in a couple of days. We go through all her scenes in the script together, following the line, talking them out, building the character development. We agree there are

changes to be made, and the kinds of changes that don't necessarily mean more space.

I speak to my grandmother, in South Africa. She's panicked because there have been headlines in the press there: 'FILMING OF SLOVO FAMILY TO BEGIN SHORTLY' in the Johannesburg Star, 'SLOVO'S DAUGHTER TELLS HER STORY' another. 'Politically aware South Africans will see the parallel between the family in the film and the real-life drama of the Slovo family. The final clue lies in the name of the writer of the film, the daughter of Joe Slovo, secretary general of the South African Communist Party and his wife, Ruth First.' This, in spite of our strategy, formulated with the Ministry in Zimbabwe, to play down the politics in the film and to stress the mother–daughter aspect of the script. My grandmother is convinced they're going to deport her. She wants to know if I can find a place for her to go. I tell her I'll phone her tomorrow.

The first dialogue scene between Diana and Molly. I'm devastated when Chris takes me aside to say he's cut a part of the action. It's not an arbitrary decision and I understand his reasons, but I panic that a vital element will be lost. Caroline warns me not to interfere: the director is in charge, the work is now his. I agree with her in theory – up to a point – but go off to mourn my loss of control in private.

17 JUNE
Chris and I rewrite a scene over lunch. I'm prickly and defensive to start with, but in the end I see why it's better. We discuss a way for me to be on set. He wants me around all the time to call on, but not necessarily right there, in his eyeline. We agree that he should rehearse on his own, and that I should come on to the floor for the first take. Then he and I will talk. He asks me not to speak to Jodhi about any of her scenes without his consent. I decide I should have a trailer, on the set, so that I can work in between being on call on Solomon's speech and the Final Confrontation and everything else that comes up. Caroline says there are no trailers left in the country. Rory tells us how many trailers there were on *Cry Freedom*. I ask around, and find one anyway.

The first day on set for Mimi and Carolyn, who play Molly's younger sisters. It's a tightly scripted scene, and by the tenth take it's obvious we have a problem with Carolyn. It's a combination of memory and timing, which is hardly surprising as she's five years old and has never acted before. At the wrap, I have a feeling this scene will not see the light of day.

## 18 JUNE

Tim Roth (Harold) flies in. He's not happy about Harold. He wants some changes made. Harold should be better delineated, more involved, have more presence. In other words, and what I hear, Harold needs more screen time. I've nothing against this in theory, but at this stage what we gain we have to lose elsewhere.

## 19 JUNE

A severe weather change: from balmy blue skies to fierce wind. A raid in the hotel for extra blankets. I phone my grandmother – she's feeling much calmer now.

My trailer's installed. Rory immediately moves in – he needs somewhere to do his paperwork. I send for my typewriter and then can't concentrate because Stuart Meachem (the Dresser) is fitting Tim Roth in the wardrobe trailer that backs on to mine.

I'm acting reluctantly as half a unit publicist on the shoot. Sarah does all the liaising with media requests which, in the light of our low-profile strategy, in effect means saying as little as possible to everyone. My task is in-depth interviews with members of the cast. Jeroen has finished his stint, just waiting for rushes clearance before he flies home to Amsterdam. We find a quiet spot in the garden. I ask him why an actor of his stature agreed to play such a small part. 'Small parts don't exist,' he says. 'Only small actors.' I ask him how he finds low-budget location pictures, and he rhapsodizes about the luxury of the Bond film before this: the de luxe food and accommodation, the chauffeur-driven cars on 24-hour standby for all the actors, in-house masseurs and physiotherapists, planes standing by to ferry people and stuff in and out. Tongue in cheek, I ask him his favourite colour and pop-star. Blue-turquoise and Rod Stewart, he answers, without batting an eyelid.

Barbara and Chris very anxious about the Final Confrontation. It's scheduled for next week, and she and Jodhi need some time with the words.

## 20 JUNE

I get a message that my father is in the vicinity, and will be flying in from Harare for a brief 36-hour visit, arriving tomorrow. Chris visibly blanches at the news. I huddle with Sarah, and we decide, in the light of the great security panic, that no one must know about this visit. In particular, we must keep it from the member of the unit we've pinpointed, after much speculation, as the security man on this picture, to prevent word getting back to Harare.

## 21 JUNE

Jeremy accompanies me to meet Joe's plane. He was about to drive Susie Figgis to the ruins at Great Zimbabwe for regeneration. Susie will not easily forgive me for causing a delay. When Joe walks off the plane, the passenger directly behind him is the member of the unit in charge of security.

Dinner with Barbara, the first time she and Joe have met. They're in a huddle all evening, at their end of the table. He asks her what she's doing after this, and for a moment she misunderstands. 'You mean this evening?' He'll dine out on that for a while.

## 22 JUNE

I try and get Joe to help with Solomon's speech. It doesn't work: he's much too interested in the filming. He wants to look through the camera, wear clothes from Wardrobe, get a haircut in the make-up trailer. Just before he leaves, he talks to me about how I have to use Solomon's speech as a vehicle to explain the tactical change in ANC policy at this time, and the background to the armed struggle. He won't give me the words though.

I try and bribe Guy Travers (1st Assistant Director) to re-schedule the Final Confrontation to give me more time. He's not a hard man, but he won't bite. I go back to the hotel, close the door, and bash it out. It turns out it was there all the time, just waiting for the last moment. I fine-tune it with Chris and Barbara, make some final changes, and issue it as pink pages.

Barney Simon flies in from Johannesburg, for a few days' visit. He tells me not to worry about Solomon's speech. He promises to sit down with me on it before he leaves.

Chris memos production, wondering whether they've tracked down the crow and the butterfly.

## 24 JUNE

Linda Mvusi's (Elsie) first day. She's wearing a maid's uniform for the action. A local white Zimbabwean watching turns to me and says, 'You could have used our maid to play this part. You would have saved on the uniform – she could have worn her own.' I take a certain satisfaction in telling him that Linda's an architect actually.

## 26 JUNE

We shoot the scene where Diana reads a letter from Gus to the children. It was originally set outside, on the patio, over lunch. We relocate it in the kitchen, with the children baking jam tarts. This activity makes the sequence far less static. In addition, we make the point that Diana is not the kind of white South African madam who never enters the servants' domain.

We find a way to work around the problem Carolyn (Miriam) is having with her dialogue. I'm detailed to hang out with the children in the school-room trailer, and to engage them in rambling and endless conversation. As soon as I hear something that will fit, I work with them on the story, so that it will fit the scene in question. It works.

## 27 AND 28 JUNE

A rest weekend. It's a fight to get on one of the two tennis courts: with every delivery of the rushes there's a racquet from home for one member of the unit or other. It's become a regular feature, with the aim of beating Pete Biziou, the top player when Graham Bradstreet isn't around. I go riding with the horsewomen of the unit, Judy Freeman (Sound Recordist) and Karen Brooks (Production Buyer). On the homeward stretch the horses bolt. I owe my life to Karen who effected a highly dramatic rescue. After X-rays at the hospital they give me a phial of green capsule painkillers. They're the same pills prescribed for every ailment by Thandile, the unit nurse, and they put you to sleep for two days. I throw them away and start treatment with the osteopath in town.

## 29 JUNE

A memo from Production. We are now seventeen minutes over our budget estimate. At this stage we can't see what we can lose in the schedule. Though it's foolish to count on it, we can only hope and pray that there'll be a significant natural fall-out in the editing process.

I advance-memo the casting department on some of the extras for the bus boycott scene. To match Diana's dialogue, we need 'spindly-legged youngsters, a sprinkling of the lame, many balancing heavy loads on their heads'. And – I can't resist it – 'mothers with babies tied securely to their backs'.

Jeremy and Andrew are having trouble finding enough white extras for the Abelson party scene, scheduled as a night shoot next week. They've used up all those sympathetic to the story for the Roth party scene. With the coverage we're getting in the *Bulawayo Chronicle* and in the South African newspapers, it's hard to maintain our front that this is a non-political mother–daughter story. Again, it's not so much that people are hostile. Living in a Frontline state, they're fearful of reprisals from white South Africa.

30 JUNE
Joyce marches in to my office, waving my casting memo. Neither of us will budge on the 'mothers with babies tied securely to their backs' issue.

Barney and I have a head-bashing session over Solomon's speech. Though it's too long, Albee feels comfortable with it, and fine-tunes it with us. (It's just as well it was never in the script – we'd never have raised the money.)

1 JULY
We film the Final Confrontation. I listen in, hidden. When we wrap, it feels as if the shooting's over.

Linda Mvusi takes me aside. She cannot play the death of Solomon, scheduled in two days' time, as written. (This is a scene where Thandile, Solomon's wife, comes to the Roth house to tell Elsie about his death.) There is no way, she says, that Thandile would be traipsing around the white suburbs to bring the news to Elsie. She would be at home, with her family, in purdah. Also, she, Linda/Elsie, will not accept comfort from Diana who, in the script, runs out to hug her. She would be too angry and too distraught to be able to be consoled by a white woman. I have a minor crisis because, in effect, I stand accused of racism. In the end, I know she's right on both points. I rewrite the sequence.

## 3 JULY

Tim Roth wonders what's happening on Harold. I've expanded the scene in the office, given him more dialogue. I've written him into the church hall meeting scene when Solomon is arrested. He wants to be at the funeral. You are at the funeral, I say. No, he doesn't want to be standing around the graveside with the women. He wants to be in the action, with the rock-throwing breakaway group who confront the security forces. Yours would be the only white face, I point out. Why is that wrong, he asks. Because it is, in the context and for the time. Don't worry, says Chris in an aside, we won't see him, I promise. Then why should he be there in the first place?

## 4 JULY

A report on the film in the *Bulawayo Bulletin*. Sarah is quoted as stressing that 'neither Shawn Slovo or myself are politically motivated, so the film will have no message'. The South Africans in the unit who closely identify with the liberation struggle are highly offended. Sarah explains that we're deliberately playing the politics down in the context of our low-profile brief, and that anyway she was misquoted. In the fall-out over the article, Sarah vows never to do another interview for the duration of filming and resigns as official Unit Publicist.

## 6 AND 7 JULY

The first night shoots. The Roth party. The temperature's hovering on freezing. Andrew and Jeremy are detailed not to let the pennywhistle-player out of their sight. I present Chris with the incidental dialogue he'd requested months ago. He's got his hands full with choreographing all the different action and clearly doesn't need it. I go back to base at a respectable hour and miss all the drama.

## 8 JULY

An unearthly stillness all day at the hotel, skull and crossbones tacked on to the doors of the rooms. The hotel have rearranged their cleaning shifts to fit in with our night shooting. The other guests are not amused.

Jeremy and Andrew try and persuade Sarah and me to appear as extras in the Abelson party scene. We refuse point blank.

## 9 JULY

We shoot the scene of Molly's point of view of her best friend, Yvonne, fooling around with her new best friend in the swimming pool. Rory tells us that on *Cry Freedom*, when they needed kids in the pool, shooting at the same time of year, the full complement of the Art and Location departments stayed up all night devising ways of heating the water. We make do with hot towels in between takes.

## 10 JULY

Our first casting disaster in the kitchen scene at the Abelson party, shooting day for night. The woman who's been cast to play Peggy, the Abelson domestic servant, can't say her lines. Hers are important words: this is the only place in the script where we hear Molly's parents' political commitment referred to by black South Africans. It's crucial for the politics of the whole. Jeremy has gone missing. We consider changing Peggy's sex and have Isaac Mabhikwa (3rd Assistant Director) stand in but, because he's also a stuntman, he's been cast to play the man on the bicycle in the accident scene. In the end, Sarah runs back to the hotel to snatch Theresa from the laundry department to step in as Peggy.

## 14 JULY

Another disaster for my children's dialogue. This time in the scene where Molly squabbles with Miriam in the car. Bertha's driving – they're on their way home, to find Diana is being arrested under the Ninety-Day Detention Act. The same problem: the children's conversation sounds laboured and trite. It's important dialogue, because it diverts the audience for a while – a calculated touch of lightness so that the arrest will have more of an impact. Neither Chris nor I are prepared – he's caught in a schedule now wherein it's become increasingly difficult to plan ahead. After take after take it's obvious the scene's not going to work.

## 15 JULY

The Abelson party scene. It's a stunning location – the achievements of Brian Morris and the Art and Construction departments on their minuscule budget never fail to amaze and impress. Somehow, in an ingenious mix of deliberate misinformation, vagueness and the promise of a night of fun, Andrew and Jeremy have delivered their quota of white party guests. As the night goes on, in freezing temperatures, neither are anywhere to be found.

As in the Roth party, there's obviously no room for the incidental dialogue I've written for the party guests. Two women have spent a week rehearsing a scripted conversation Molly overhears. By the time Chris gets around to shooting it they're both too drunk to deliver. The light's gone anyway.

A member of crew (not working) is so carried away by the party spirit that he lunges at Kate Fitzpatrick (June Abelson), falling on top of her into a flowerbed. The osteopath is called in to work on her shoulder.

## 16 JULY
Diana's narrow escape from arrest – another night shoot. Chris has sneaked in some extra – unscripted – action here. He wants the audience to see the arrested men being led out of the building. I wonder why. (In the end, it's not on the screen.)

## 19 JULY
I issue the rewritten prison interrogation scenes as pink pages. There's more there than I'm at ease with.

## 20 JULY
Out into the streets of downtown Bulawayo. Rory's in a sulk because he hasn't got enough tape for crowd control barriers. We don't even need it – though crowds gather wherever we film, they only want to watch. They stay put where they're placed. We shoot the scene where the African is knocked down by a white hit-and-run driver. Isaac plays the African. One of the cars, driving past as he lies in the road, runs over his hand. He's only bruised, but drama occurs when he jumps to his feet and chases after the white driver, screaming that it was done on purpose. He has to be restrained.

We have to reschedule the second set-up of the day – June picking up Molly and Yvonne from the Spanish dancing class – when her action vehicle, already established, breaks down. It's not only that it's a twenty-five-year-old car – it's virtually impossible to find parts and spares in Zimbabwe.

## 21 JULY
The scene where Diana's office has been searched and ransacked by the security forces. Neville Rhodes, the standby painter, is

23

summoned to put a hammer and sickle in red on the wall. There's an endless debate about which way round it goes.

Later, a rehearsal of the office scene to be shot tomorrow. As written, when the radio announces the introduction of the Ninety-Day Act, there's a reaction shot from all three principals – Diana, Harold, Saeeda. What they feel, the fear, the uncertainty of the times, is in their faces. Barbara wants to add a line. I think it's superfluous. Chris is keeping out of this one. Stalemate.

## 22 JULY

Barbara gets to say her line. In the second set-up, the conversation between Diana and Molly as they leave the office building, Chris asks Barbara to link arms with her daughter. I hear her over the headphones: 'That's not how Ruth First would have done it.' She could be right – it's the way I would have wanted my mother to have done it.

Mike Proudfoot, the Camera Operator, is bent over all day, can't stand up. He's sent to the osteopath.

## 23 JULY

We move on and into the prison location. It's been constructed underneath the grandstands of a football stadium in Bulawayo's state fairground and it's been a race against time for Brian and the boys to get it ready. This because Chris held out until the last moment for a real prison – he wouldn't accept when it was made clear to us from the beginning that we would never be given permission.

I'm agitated and concerned about some of the extra words for these prison interrogation scenes. I'll talk to anybody who'll listen about the length problem we're compounding, and the danger to Molly's point of view. Finally, and negotiated by Sarah, I agree to keep out of the way while the interrogations are being filmed.

Chris sends another memo about the black crow he needs for a scene tomorrow. No one thought he was serious. Chris Thompson (2nd Assistant Director) swings into action.

## 24 JULY

'ANY TAMED CROW AROUND' reads the front-page headline of the *Bulawayo Chronicle*. It's an 'emergency request . . . vital for a scene we're shooting today . . . desperate' – Chris Thompson is quoted. With minutes to spare, a woman arrives with her pet crow in a box. We drive them out to the location. The bird's positioned in place in the prison courtyard, a few feet from Barbara who sits crouched in a corner. But it won't play. As soon as it's left alone, it makes straight for its owner, no matter what we bribe it with to stay. Chris Menges finally admits defeat. Chris Thompson pays it off and sends it home.

Maureen Stephenson, the Make-up Assistant, injures her leg. She's sent to the osteopath.


25 JULY
I interview David Suchet. He says that what attracted him to the project was the script. What else can he say, I think to myself, when the scriptwriter's doubling as unofficial unit publicist. He much prefers working on low-budget location films. With the majors, there are always five executive producers, three line producers, at least five writers, too much waste, too much tension. As an actor he feels compromised in a situation where they have the luxury to decide that if it's not OK then they can always shoot or cut around it. And the whole process, because there's so much money around, takes far too long. I wonder what a million more would have meant on our budget. You could have paid the actors more, quips David. I ask how he feels having the writer on set. He talks about how, in an ideal world, writer, director and actors should be totally collaborative in the making of the film, then circumvents the answer by saying that in most of the things he's worked on, particularly in the theatre, the writer's been dead.

We reshoot June Abelson picking up the children from Spanish dance lessons. Her car breaks down again, and by the time they've got it going we've lost the light.


26 JULY
Andrew and Jeremy can't find a handful of white anti-apartheid demonstrating extras for the scene outside the prison, to be shot tomorrow. Two middle-aged ladies had agreed to participate, then withdraw at the last moment, as they're fitted with placards saying RELEASE OUR LEADERS. They thought it was a cake-baking demonstration.

Afghan, the horse that bolted with me on his back, is dead. Kidney failure and a heart attack. I have to laugh at the conspiracy to keep the news from me for a while: they thought I'd be distraught.

## 27 JULY
I lose my office. (I lost my trailer weeks ago.) We're about to shoot the major crowd scenes – the bus boycott and the funeral – and Make-up and Hair need more space. I couldn't wish for a more pleasant pair of room-mates than Elaine Carew and Maureen, but it's hard to concentrate amidst the bottles of blood, the smell of hair dye, and Barbara's wig. It's an unmistakable sign that the rewriting is virtually over. As the writer, I experience a certain loss of power and status.

## 29 JULY
I play a woman prisoner extra, in the scene where Diana is released, before she's re-arrested on the street. Only to help Jeremy and Andrew out. (It doesn't make it to the final cut. In fact, it wasn't even in the rushes.)

## 30 JULY
The visit to the prison by the children. For the first time, Carolyn gets the scripted dialogue right. It's a scene in the script that's very close to the way it was and I'm moved by the action. I've deliberately tried to view all this from a distance, as separate from my own experience, but it sometimes crosses over.

I rewrite Diana's suicide note. I don't stop to think about this task – rewriting my own mother's suicide note.

## 1 AUGUST
The final interrogation scene, the one where Diana gives a statement. When that statement is exposed, she realizes she can't get away with withholding information any longer. In the scene after this, she attempts suicide. I can't keep away from the shooting and watch from a respectable distance. David Suchet (Muller) has a problem with the scene: he feels the lead-in is terribly short. I feel, and from the way it's written, the audience will know that we come into it in the middle of the scene. Barbara says she's playing the scene as if it begins in the beginning. That's not the way it was written, I say. Sarah drives me back to the hotel. We pick up a packed lunch, a bottle of champagne, and a Holiday

26

Inn dustbin filled with ice, and head out to the Matopas. We picnic at the reservoir, and score points by seeing white rhino. By the end of the day, I'm over my tantrum.

## 2 AUGUST

We're working a day at weekends now in the race against time which is money. We finally get the shot of June Abelson picking up the children from the Spanish dance class. The owner of her car swears he will never get involved in this kind of thing again.

## 3 AUGUST

Interior of church. Solomon's funeral, an event which has a particular poignancy for many of those involved, principals and extras who have lost family and friends in the struggle against apartheid. A day of high drama: the singing is so powerful, the action so realistic that quite a few of the participants are overcome with emotion.

## 5 AUGUST

To the township, to shoot the chicken-foot-in-the-soup scene at the location for Solomon's house. The family whose home it is are in seventh heaven. Brian has designed the extension we need to be permanent. It almost doubles the size of the house, and that's two years' wages in these parts.

The old blind man who plays Elsie's and Solomon's grandfather is completely disoriented by the process. He's plied with tea in the interminable delays involved in setting up. By the time we come to shoot the scene, he needs to be led away to the bathroom every ten minutes. As Chris has chosen to film this in one set-up, it's not great for continuity.

## 6 AUGUST

The final scene in the film – Solomon's funeral procession, the priest's sermon at the graveside, the arrival of the security forces. Chris is depressed that he's only got 1400 extras. Sarah isn't even prepared to discuss it at this stage.

In the chaos of a long and windy day, the crowd is supportive and patient. Throughout the nine-week shooting period, the spirit of cooperation and involvement on the part of the people of Bulawayo has been remarkable.

I spot Harold (Tim Roth) in the breakaway militant group the crowd. He's running with them, throwing rocks. The only white face. Chris is too exhausted to take him on. Don't worry, he assures me again, we'll never see him on screen. (You have to be quick, but he's there . . .)

## 7 AUGUST
A marathon interview with Kate Fitzpatrick (June Abelson). We talk in depth about the character she plays, and the Junes we've both known – pretty girls who marry rich men and live in beautiful houses and never do any housework. The kind of woman who says, 'I can't understand what all this black and white problem's about. I mean, I have a black nanny that I've always loved, she was my sister's nanny and my brother's nanny, she's been in our family for fifty years and now she doesn't work any more and she just lives in a beautiful house we pay for and we always send her flowers on her birthday and everything. I don't understand what everybody's going on about, I've never had any problems.' And if June's daughter hadn't been Molly's best friend, if she hadn't met the Roths, then she wouldn't ever have had to look outside her front door. And if her husband, Gerald, leaves her no room to manoeuvre, then it doesn't make her less guilty. June and Gerald can't believe in anything outside themselves, because it would contradict and interfere too much. She rhapsodizes over Chris as a director. What he's achieved is to cast the film so perfectly. And he trusts the actors to deliver. He made her feel both free and safe at the same time. 'If it was indulgent or bad then he would stop me. Other than that, he knows what's right and if it's right for him, then it's right for me. I'd work for him for nothing.'

## 8 AUGUST
I interview Jude Akuwidike, who plays the priest. When I play it back later, the tape's blank. It didn't take. I can't bring myself to tell Sarah. I've had it with being unofficial unit publicist.

The osteopath has had a heart attack.

## 9 AUGUST
The unit's exhausted, stir-crazy and trying to get away from each other. There's a mass exodus from the hotel for the day but we all meet up in the Matopas anyway.

## 10 AUGUST

We film the bus boycott scene. There are babies tied securely to their mother's backs. Joyce is hardly talking to me.

## 11 AUGUST

Less than four days to finish off at the school. Jodhi (Molly) and Nadine (Yvonne) are barely talking to each other by now which makes it difficult.

I watch my favourite scene – Harold with Molly at the school, after Diana's re-arrest. I'm horrified when Tim Roth wants to play it sitting down, on the ground. I know this is a scene that must be played standing up. We shoot it both ways.

## 12 AUGUST

We shoot the dreaded classroom history-lesson scene, where Chris wants the butterfly. As Lloyd has long since departed the film, his elaborate scheme via the museum came to nought. Word has been spread through the townships, and in the morning there's a line of small boys holding boxes containing butterflies. Most of them are dead and we kill a few more before Chris is satisfied.

## 13 AUGUST

In the evening, Chris gets to shoot the train sequence that we argued over so. This is one of the ways Chris planned to open out the film. I'm all for that in theory, but I can't see how this will work for us – it comes from nowhere and we don't follow it through. I stay away in protest.

## 14 AUGUST

The last day of principal photography. In the high spirits after the final wrap, I'm the only woman to get dunked in the champagne ice bath.

## 15 AUGUST

The wrap party. In the lead-up, a split between those who want to hold it at the hotel base, and those who think it would be more of an event to have it in town. Because Sarah's in the town faction, we win. Volunteers spend the day dressing and lighting the hall. Jeremy goes for flowers – something of a mission in drought-ridden Bulawayo – and goes missing for the rest of the day.

It's a disaster. By the time the unit arrives – those who aren't boycotting it because it's not at the hotel – the hall is filled to capacity by what appears to be the whole of Bulawayo and regions beyond. The free bar is over an hour after the doors open, the corridors lined with the unconscious. We empty the hall and try and start again, but no one can get through the crowds outside. The Sparks are having their own party at the hotel. Stuart Monteith is summoned from sleep to amuse us with Continuity and Sound impersonations.

## 17 AUGUST

A card to the unit from Phyllis Naidoo (Saeeda). 'I was reluctantly persuaded to take part in this film. I thank all of you for this valuable experience. I am convinced that success can never be the preserve of a single body. It belongs to all – your corporate skills make it possible and this includes the dishwashers, the sweepers, the laundry women. Consciously or otherwise, we have all been involved for Ruth and for the struggle in South Africa that she gave her all.'

Today is the fifth anniversary of Ruth's assassination.

## 13 OCTOBER

Jeremy Brickhill is badly wounded by a car-bomb attack in Harare, near his home. His injuries will take years to heal, and he will never fully recover his health.

The bomb was planted and detonated by agents of the South African racist regime. The perpetrators have been caught, and their trial in Zimbabwe will reveal how Jeremy was under surveillance by his attackers for months before the incident. That would include the period of the filming, when the security precautions we were forced to take seemed at times unnecessary and over-dramatic.

### Epilogue

The debate about the title continued through production and post-production. We could never agree on a replacement, so *A World Apart* it is.

The final cut has been screened in Los Angeles, New York and London. It was screened at the Cannes Film Festival and won the

Special Jury Prize and Jodhi, Barbara and Linda Mvusi together won the Best Actress Award. It has been sold world-wide, though not in South Africa.

In the editing process, weaknesses in parts of the script were exposed: a failure in plotting I was always aware of but never dealt with properly, hoping it wouldn't show. Hopefully, the cutting covers this up, but what the experience has reinforced is the absolute priority to get the script right before you start.

I've been proved both right and wrong in the battle of the prison interrogations. As the writer, I'm proud of the fact that the dialogue and the structure and scene continuity, from the page to the screen, has largely stood the test of the process. I regret some of what we've had to lose, particularly the bulk of the June Abelson subplot. It's not so much that it was crucial to the plot, but we fought for it for the texture of white South African life it adds. We just didn't have the space to contain it in the end. I've only myself to blame – the script was always too long.

In the end, the way Chris filmed the younger children, and in particular in the reactions he coaxed from them, belies the crisis over the difficulties they had with the dialogue. Chris took what was on the page and made it stronger.

I may have given the impression that I often experienced it as interference, but in the end I have nothing but respect and thanks for the part the actors played. In their individual attempts to centre themselves in their roles, they gave the story life and texture.

Through being involved in the process – and particularly as a member of the unit during the filming – I've learnt an enormous amount about writing for the screen. Consistent with the respect Chris and Sarah have shown from the beginning, I was consulted and referred to throughout the editing process. I've seen the way film-writers are treated. I've been spoilt for life.

Shawn Slovo
London, June 1988

31

*A World Apart* opened at the Curzon Cinema on 26 August 1988. The cast included:

| | |
|---|---|
| DIANA | Barbara Hershey |
| MOLLY | Jodhi May |
| MULLER | David Suchet |
| GUS | Jeroen Krabbe |
| BERTHA | Yvonne Bryceland |
| MRS HARRIS | Rosalie Crutchley |
| KRUGER | Paul Freeman |
| SOLOMON | Albee Lesotho |
| ELSIE | Linda Mvusi |
| HAROLD | Tim Roth |
| | |
| *Casting* | Susie Figgis |
| *Director of Photography* | Peter Biziou |
| *Art Director* | Brian Morris |
| *Costume Designer* | Nic Ede |
| *Sound* | Judy Freeman |
| *Editor* | Nicolas Gaster |
| *Music* | Hans Zimmer |
| *Script* | Shawn Slovo |
| *Producer* | Sarah Radclyffe |
| *Director* | Chris Menges |

A Working Title production
Stills by David Appleby

## SOUTH AFRICA, 1963

1. EXT. ROTH HOUSE. NIGHT
*Night sounds of the southern hemisphere. The Roth family house. A light shines from one of the bedrooms. A car parked in the driveway.*

2. INT. ROTH HOUSE. PANTRY. NIGHT
*Moonlight reflected as* MOLLY ROTH, *thirteen years old, in her dressing gown, drinks a glass of water.*

3. INT. CORRIDOR. NIGHT
MOLLY *walks quietly down the corridor. Off screen the sounds of rustling, muted voices, laughter. She stops outside the half-open door to her parent's bedroom. What she sees:*

4. INT. GUS AND DIANA ROTH'S BEDROOM. NIGHT
GUS and DIANA ROTH, *Molly's parents, in their mid thirties. She's in her nightgown, he's in the final stages of dressing. He reaches out to her, takes her in his arms. They kiss.*

### 5. INT. CORRIDOR. NIGHT

MOLLY *turns and walks quietly back down the corridor.*

### 6. INT. MOLLY'S ROOM. NIGHT

MOLLY *lies in bed.* GUS *comes into the room, kneels by the side of the bed.*

GUS: I've come to say goodbye. I have to go away for a while.

MOLLY: Where are you going?

GUS: Some place . . .

MOLLY: When will you be coming back?

GUS: I don't know. A few weeks, maybe a month.

MOLLY: Are you going out of the country?

GUS: Molly. Enough. It's my work. You know I can't talk about it.

    (*He ruffles her hair.*)

    You'll hear from me, I promise. I love you very much. Be cheerful, my honey.

    (*He hugs her tightly, then gets up, walks away.*)

MOLLY: Dad. Wish me luck.

    (GUS *looks puzzled for a moment.*)

GUS: Oh, yes. Good luck.

    (*He strikes a flamenco pose, clicks his fingers.*)

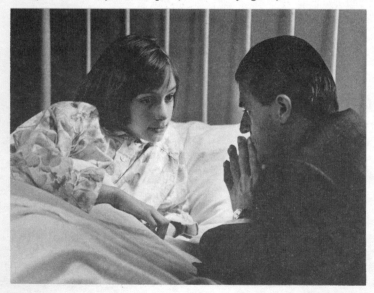

Olé!
(MOLLY *giggles.* GUS *leaves.*)

7. EXT. CORRIDOR/SITTING ROOM. NIGHT
MOLLY *runs quickly down the corridor to the sitting-room window.*
*She parts the curtain, looks out. What she sees:*

8. EXT. DRIVEWAY. NIGHT
GUS and DIANA *walk arm in arm to the car. He gets into the car.*
*She reaches in to hold him for a moment, then stands back as he*
*reverses away. She looks after the empty driveway.*

9. INT. SPANISH DANCE CLASS. DAY
*An ageing heavily made-up 'Spanish' dance* TEACHER *claps her*
*hands loudly together, stamps her feet.* MOLLY *is in the class of*
*about ten children, following her moves. The* TEACHER *shouts out*
*the rhythm, an instruction, a reprimand. She turns off the music.*

TEACHER: That's it. Thank you. See you next week. Molly,
 Yvonne, let me see your routine.
 (MOLLY *and* YVONNE ABELSON, *also thirteen, face each
 other, raise their arms.*)
 *Uno, dos, tres . . .*
 (*They dance. They're not very good, but they're completely into
 it.*)


## 10. EXT. CITY STREET. DAY

MOLLY *and* YVONNE, *flushed, emerge from the building, blink in
the sunlight of a cloudless day.*
*White men and women, smartly dressed, walk purposefully down the
street. They're outnumbered by Africans, mainly men, on foot and on
bicycles. Some in old-fashioned, ill-fitting suits, others in overalls
and work-clothes, a few in rags or a blanket, barefoot. The women
balance heavy loads on their heads. The road-sweepers are black,
and a black child mans the newspaper stand. The headlines: '90
DAY ACT BECOMES LAW'.*
*A car horn sounds impatiently, and an open cadillac pulls into the
kerb.* JUNE ABELSON *is at the wheel – mid-thirties, deeply tanned,
heavily bejewelled, headscarf, dark glasses, red mouth. A dog on the
seat next to her, barking.*
*She leans over to open the door.* MOLLY *lingers.*
MOLLY: I'm going to my mother's office.
JUNE: Get in. I'll drop you there.
MOLLY: It's only around the corner.
JUNE: You can't walk on your own. Come on, get in.
 (MOLLY *gets into the back next to* YVONNE *who barks back at
 the dog.*)
 Stop it, Yvonne. You make him crazy.
 (*She executes a U-turn, stopping the oncoming traffic with red
 varnished nails.*
 MOLLY *and* YVONNE *in the back, playing a silly hand-
 clapping rhyming game, giggling.*
 JUNE *slams on the brakes as the car in front hits a black
 cyclist, emerging from an intersection. Hardly pausing, the
 driver accelerates and roars off.*
 *Some blacks run after the car, shouting. Others gather around
 the cyclist who lies in the road, bleeding heavily. There's a lot
 of shouting and arguing, in various languages. Any whites on*

the street go out of their way to avoid the scene, save for one old
woman who pushes her way through the crowd to attend to the
man. She takes charge. Passing cars slow, peer curiously, drive
on. The dog's really barking.)
Oh, shut up.
(They watch as the crowd argues.)
(Shouting) Don't move him! Call an ambulance!
(MOLLY looks at her, hesitates.)
MOLLY: Why don't we take him?
JUNE: No. I don't want to get involved.
(An AFRICAN MAN looks daggers at them, says something in
his own language.)
(Loudly) Hey! (Low) It's not my fault. I didn't do it!
(The AFRICAN MAN stares back at her contemptuously.)
AFRICAN MAN: You people are all the same.
(A couple of men in the crowd pick up the cyclist and carry him
across the street to a battered car. The crowd follows, still

*arguing, a couple of women's voices raised angrily above the rest.*

*Her way clear,* JUNE *drives off.* MOLLY *turns back to look at the remains of the mangled bike at the side of the road.)*

11. INT. DIANA'S NEWSPAPER OFFICE. DAY
*A large, cluttered room, tables loaded with papers and bundles of newspapers. Resistance posters cover the walls, photographs are pinned in their groupings on every available surface.*
*In one corner is a huge Xerox machine, operated by a young Indian woman,* SAEEDA. HAROLD, *a white man in his thirites, types furiously at one of the desks.* DIANA, *stylishly dressed, at another desk. She's dictating over the telephone, her words just audible in the din of the Xerox machine and typewriter.*
MOLLY *wanders through the room, at home here, sipping a soft drink noisily through a straw. She picks up a leaflet from the pile on the floor. It's a reduced copy of one of the posters predominant on the walls: a black and white photograph of a group of arrested Africans with the caption: 'PROTEST WITH US AGAINST THE PASS LAWS'. She surreptitiously folds it, puts it in her pocket.*
HAROLD *looks up at her from his typing.*
HAROLD: So. How's school?

MOLLY: (*Polite*) Fine, thank you.

HAROLD: That's good.

(*He goes back to his typing.*

SAEEDA *glances at the clock, stops the Xerox machine and starts turning the knobs of a large radio.*

MOLLY *stares at a group of photographs tacked to a wall: a sequence of black farm workers, herded in overcrowded barns, dressed in sackcloth in the fields, lining up for rations, whip scars on some bare torsos.*

HAROLD *stops typing momentarily.*)

DIANA: (*On phone*) '. . . Thousands of Africans are being kidnapped, shanghai'd away from the towns and their families to do enforced labour on the farms. South Africa will not have farm workers with a love and knowledge of the land until they are ensured of a living wage, adequate food, housing, education and security – and above all the freedom to enjoy the fullness of life . . .'

(MOLLY *stares at the photograph of a farm worker, sitting in his bunk amid meagre possessions, dressed in sackcloth, his hands clasped in his lap. He looks straight at the camera.*)

'. . . The farm labour scandal brings to the fore the worst features of the apartheid cheap-labour state, and gives them a new and more hideous form.' That's it. Leave three columns for the picture. Thanks. Goodbye.

(*She replaces the receiver, picks it up to re-dial.* SAEEDA *turns up the radio.* DIANA *replaces the receiver.* HAROLD *stops typing.*)

NEWSREADER: (*BBC World Service*) '. . . The South African government today announced the first arrests under the newly enacted Ninety Day Detention Act. The Act confers power on the Security Forces to detain people without trial for up to ninety days for interrogation, and follows in the wake of increased underground activity by the recently banned African National Congress. Under an agreement between Washington and Moscow, a hotline emergency link to reduce the risk of accidental nuclear war will go into service on August the thirtieth . . .'

(SAEEDA *turns off the radio. There's silence for a beat.* SAEEDA *sighs, exclaims softly.* DIANA *rubs at her eyes.* HAROLD *is angry. Then* DIANA *glances at her watch, swears, gets up hurriedly, gathering papers from her desk.*)

DIANA: Molly, let's go. (*To* HAROLD) Could you drop that off at the house this afternoon –

HAROLD: Jesus, Diana. I made a promise to my kids, Marge has made arrangements –

DIANA: (*Angry*) You promised *me* that report three days ago. I'm going to have to work on it over the weekend . . . (HAROLD *looks furious.*)
Don't make *me* feel bad about this, Harold.
(*She stares at him. He glares back at her for a beat, then looks away.*)
I'll see you, Saeeda.
(SAEEDA *waves goodbye.* DIANA *walks out, followed by* MOLLY.)

MOLLY: You promised we'd get the lace today.

## 12. INT. NEWSPAPER OFFICE. CORRIDOR/STAIRS. DAY

DIANA: Darling, there's no time. I'll drop you off at the store. You can meet me at the hairdresser.

MOLLY: I need you to help me. The competition's on Tuesday.

DIANA: Then you'll have to wait. I'll treat you to a hairdo. How about that?
(*A pause.* DIANA *checking through her briefcase as they descend the stairway.*)

MOLLY: Mom, there was an accident on the corner of Jeppe Street. It was a black man. A black man on a bicycle –
(DIANA *stops, swears softly under her breath.*)

DIANA: Damn. I've left something behind. Here. I'll meet you at the car.
(*She hands* MOLLY *the keys, turns to dash back up the stairs.*)

## 13. INT. DIANA'S CAR. DAY

*The car turns into the Roth driveway from the street. They've both been to the hairdresser.*

MOLLY: . . . I *need* it. I have to have it. Yvonne's mother took her *ages* ago –

DIANA: Yvonne's mother's got nothing else to do. And why didn't she get some lace for you?

MOLLY: Why should she? She's not my mother, you're my mother.

42

## 14. EXT. ROTH HOUSE. DRIVEWAY. DAY

*Molly's sisters,* JUDE, *eight, and* MIRIAM, *six, run out from the house to meet them.*

MIRIAM: (*Angry*) Why are you so late? The chips are burned! The chips are burned!

    (JUDE *stares at* MOLLY.)

JUDE: What happened to your hair?

MOLLY: It's a hairdo, you stupid.


## 15. INT. MOLLY'S ROOM. DAY

MOLLY *comes in, closes the door. She opens the closet, gets down on her knees and pulls out a box file. It's discretely secure. Inside are newspaper articles and photographs of Gus and Diana, all in connection with their political activities throughout the past decade. She slips the leaflet she took from the office into the box, closes the closet door.*
*She sneaks a look at her hair in the mirror. She touches it tentatively, uncertain.*


## 16. INT. KITCHEN. DAY

ELSIE, *a strong, large African woman in her twenties, preparing lunch.*

MOLLY: Ahem.

    (ELSIE *turns, looks at* MOLLY *in the doorway, exclaims.*)

    I went to the hairdresser. Do you like it?

    (*A pause.*)

ELSIE: It's . . . nice. But what did they do to your curls?

    (MOLLY *flounces out of the room.*)


## 17. EXT. ROTH VERANDA. DAY

DIANA *and the children on the veranda. The remains of lunch on the table.* MOLLY *has washed out her hairdo.* DIANA *reading from a letter.*

DIANA: (*Scanning*) '. . . this is for me . . . Ah, here: "As for you three girls, I miss you all terribly. It's unbearably hot here and I long for the beach at Cape Town, and our Sundays by the swimming pool. Molly, good luck! *Ole!* Jude, those were excellent exam marks. And, Miriam, thank you – " '

MIRIAM: Here's Gran!

(*She runs to meet a car turning into the driveway.* BERTHA, *Diana's mother, the children's grandmother, at the wheel. She misjudges the circular driveway and collides with the dustbins. She gets out of the car.*)

BERTHA: They were in the way. Why do you always leave the dustbins in that place . . .

(DIANA *gives her a look.* MIRIAM *jumps into her arms, hugging her.*)

MIRIAM: Gran, we got a letter from Daddy. Gran, I want to show you something, in my room . . .

(MILIUS, *Elsie's husband, the gardener and cook, comes out from the backyard, picks up the dustbins.*)

BERTHA: Thank you, Milius. There are oranges, and biscuits, in the back –

DIANA: Mom, you brought a sack last week. There are oranges on the tree . . .

(BERTHA, *carrying* MIRIAM, *steps on to the veranda. She kisses* JUDE *and* MOLLY.)

BERTHA: Hello, darling, hello, darling. Molly, you shouldn't sit around with wet hair, you'll get pneumonia. (*To* DIANA, *lowered tone*) Is he well? Is there news?

MOLLY: Mom, finish the letter –

(MIRIAM, *tugging at* BERTHA.)

MIRIAM: Gran. I want to show you something. In my room. Come, Gran –

DIANA: Mom, I have to be out of town on Wednesday. Could you collect the kids –

JUDE: Mom, I've got riding on Wednesday –

BERTHA: I've made plans. I'll have to cancel them –

DIANA: No. It's all right. I'll find someone else –

BERTHA: It's OK, Diana. It's only a gallery opening. I don't have to go on that day –

DIANA: Mom, if you've made plans then it doesn't matter –

BERTHA: My plans aren't important. I'll do it.

(*A pause. This friction between them is history.*)

MOLLY: Mom, the letter . . .

DIANA: (*Reading*) '. . . and Miriam, thank you for your letter of seventy-three kisses – I've never had one quite like it. Write to me all of you. Keep happy, hugs and kisses . . .' The rest is for me.

44

(MIRIAM *pulls* BERTHA *away, into the house.*
*A pause.* MOLLY *watches as* DIANA *reads, completely*
*absorbed.*)
MOLLY: What does he say?
(DIANA *doesn't hear her.* MOLLY *gets up, walks away.*)

18. EXT. YARD. DAY
*Pan* MOLLY *from house.*

19. INT. ELSIE'S ROOM. DAY
*It's roomy and tidy, with the same curtains as in the main house and*
*furnished simply but with care. A cross on the wall, a treadle sewing*
*machine in one corner, a vase of plastic flowers. Other photographs*
*on the wall include Elsie's children, one of the Roth family, and a*
*separate one of Molly, in a swimsuit.*
ELSIE *sits at the dressing table, rubbing Vaseline into the soles of her*
*feet.* MOLLY *lolls on the bed.*
ELSIE: (*Singing*)

> 'Nkosi sikelel' i-Afrika
> Maluphakanyisw' uphondo lwayo
> Yizwa imithandazo yethu
> Nkosi sikelela – Nkosi sikelela.'

*(She stops. MOLLY raises herself on to her elbows. She sings. She loses the tune. ELSIE corrects her. MOLLY sings, stumbles over a word. ELSIE sings it. MOLLY starts again, hesitatingly, but gets through it with Elsie's help. They sing it again, ELSIE harmonizing while MOLLY holds the tune. They laugh, delighted.)*

20. INT. DIANA'S BEDROOM. NIGHT

DIANA *at her dressing-table, applying make-up.* MOLLY *sitting beside her, draping her head and neck with Diana's jewellery, sharing the mirror. She clips on a pair of large silver earrings.*

MOLLY: Mom, leave these to me in your will.

DIANA: Molly, get out of the way.

*(She bumps MOLLY, pushing her off the stool. MOLLY falls exaggeratedly to the floor. She lies there for a moment, then gets up, goes to the open wardrobe. She scrutinizes herself in the full-length mirror.)*

MOLLY: I've got good legs.

*(DIANA turns around to look at her, amused.)*

DIANA: Who told you that?

MOLLY: Oh, somebody.
>(DIANA *waits. It's obvious* MOLLY's *not going to say any*
>*more.* DIANA *turns back to her make-up.*
>MOLLY *stares at Gus's clothes in one half of the wardrobe,*
>*momentarily smells the sleeve of a jacket. She walks over to the*
>*bed, flings herself on it.* DIANA *picks out a dress from the*
>*closet, puts it on.*)
>Mom. When's he coming back?
DIANA: I don't know. He doesn't know.
MOLLY: But when do you *think* he's coming back?
>(DIANA *makes an irritated sound, searches through the bottom*
>*of the wardrobe, pulls out a pair of shoes.*)
>Mom? When do you think?
DIANA: (*Irritated*) A week. Eleven days. At the end of the
>month. I don't know, and neither does he.
>(*A pause.*)
MOLLY: (*Upset, muffled*) Well, I want him here.
DIANA: So do I. *So does he.* You know that.
>(*A pause.*)
>(*Conciliatory*) What do you think? Do these match?
>(*In spite of herself* MOLLY *looks at her mother's high-heeled*
>*shoes.*)

21. EXT. MIDTOWN STREET. RAIN. NIGHT
DIANA *parks in a main street. She gets out of the car, carrying her*
*briefcase, walks quickly towards the main entrance of an apartment*
*building. She trips, swears as her heel is caught in the pavement.*
*She slips out of the shoe, wrenches it free, wobbling off on one heel.*

22. INT. MOLLY'S BEDROOM. RAIN. NIGHT
MOLLY *suddenly awake.*

23. INT. DIANA'S BEDROOM. RAIN. NIGHT
*The bed is empty, the curtains wide open.*
MOLLY *climbs on to the dressing table and draws the curtains*
*together. She gets down and scrutinizes the length of curtains at the*
*join. There are no gaps.*

24. INT. APARTMENT BUILDING. RAIN. NIGHT
DIANA *hobbles through the lobby to the lift. She presses the button,*

*waits, examining the broken heel of her shoe. Then she glances at the
adjacent wall, starts. What she sees: a sign indicating No
Vacancies. She turns and walks quickly out of the building.*

### 25. EXT. APARTMENT BUILDING. RAIN. NIGHT
*As* DIANA *emerges* GEORGE, *an old Zulu caretaker, appears from
the shadows of the adjacent side alley. He comes towards her,
waving his arms, shooing her away.*

DIANA: George. . . ?

    (*He waves his arms frantically.*)

GEORGE: Go! Go! Quick! Go! Shoo!

DIANA: What's happened. . . ?

GEORGE: Police at the back! Go! Go!

    (DIANA *slips off her good shoe and runs across the street. She
gets to the car, glances back. What she sees: The street is quiet
and deserted save for a water howser making its slow progress
through the night.*

    *She gets into the car, drives away.*

    *Then, in the distance, police cars appear, stopping outside the
entrance to the apartment building. Police, armed and
uniformed, with dogs, enter the building.*)

26. INT. DIANA'S CAR. RAIN. NIGHT
*Sweating, her hands gripping the wheel, she drives off slowly in the opposite direction.*

27. EXT. ROTH DRIVEWAY. DAY
MOLLY, *in her school uniform, swinging on the gate. She's chewing bubble-gum, popping bubbles. In the distance, a ten-year-old black boy delivering newspapers.*
*A garbage truck passes the house. The driver is white, the garbage collectors black. They whistle and shout to each other, sing and chant as they run to keep pace with the moving truck. Every dog in the neighbourhood is barking.*
*The newspaper boy reaches the gate as* MOLLY *blows a huge bubble. He stops to watch her. It bursts, covering the lower part of her face. He laughs, she laughs, scraping it off. As he hands her the newspaper, she offers him a piece of gum. He claps his hands, then cups them in acceptance.*
MOLLY *unfolds the newspaper to the front page. What she sees: A headline: 'POLICE NET SIX AT ANC MEETING – LINK WITH BOMB BLAST KILLINGS' and a photograph of the midtown apartment building.*

28. INT. STUDY. DAY
DIANA: (*Voice-over on tape*) '. . . The prosperity of the gold-mining industry has been based on the poverty of Africa and her people. The wealth of the reef gold mines lies not in the richness of the strike but in the low costs of production, kept down by the abundance of cheap labour . . .' (DIANA *at her desk, transcribing from tape recorder to typewriter. The shutters are drawn against the sun.*) '. . . chasing down figures of mine wages is like pursuing dandelions through thick mist . . . (note to myself to check the suppressed 1960 Mines Commission Report) . . . (*She searches through the pile of papers on her desk, swears under her breath, gets up and walks around to the side of the desk.*) '. . . the majority of workers are migrants . . . a system responsible for the most blatant exploitation of the largest single labour force in South Africa . . .' (*She kneels, places her hands underneath the desk, locates something with her fingers. There's a click, and a panel swings open to reveal an*

*expertly constructed compartment, filled with papers, pamphlets,*
*technical drawings, etc. She searches through them.)*
'. . . elaborate on the disastrous social effects . . . shattered
homes . . . children deprived of adequate parenting . . .
meagre cash wage . . . no overtime or sick pay . . .'
*(The door opens.* DIANA *starts.* MOLLY, *holding the*
*newspaper.)*
DIANA: When the door is closed, you knock. I'm working. I
don't want to be interrupted.
*(She turns off the tape.* MOLLY *stares at the open panel.)*
MOLLY: Is that a hiding place?
*(*DIANA *stares at her for a beat.)*
DIANA: Yes. And you must keep it a secret. Do you
understand?
*(A pause.)*
MOLLY: What do you keep in there?
DIANA: *(Impatient)* Molly, that's enough. And brush your hair
before you go to school. What did you want?
*(*MOLLY, *trying to remember. Then she hands over the*
*newspaper.* DIANA *takes it eagerly. She scans the front page.*
MOLLY *watches her, then stares at the open compartment.*
DIANA *is absorbed.* MOLLY *leaves.)*

29. INT. SCHOOL ASSEMBLY HALL. DAY

> Uit die blou van onse hemel
> Uit die diepte van onse see, etc.

*(The assembled girls, singing the South African National*
*Anthem.*
MOLLY *stares straight ahead, her lips not moving.* YVONNE
*sings lustily next to her.)*

30. INT. MINING COMPOUND. DAY
*In the distance, about sixty black shift workers, filing out to the*
*minehead.*

31. INT. MINING COMPOUND. DAY
DIANA, *escorted through the empty corridor by a nervous* BLACK
OFFICIAL. *She talks softly into her tape recorder, describing the*

*rows of dug-out beds crammed in the huge, unlit room, the scanty*
*belongings, the dirt, the open urinal at one end, etc.*

## 32. INT. SCHOOL CHANGING ROOMS. DAY
MOLLY *and* YVONNE *rush in, late. Girls changing, chatting.*
MOLLY *at her locker. Inside finding a newspaper article. Bold*
*headline: 'GUS ROTH: WANTED FOR TREASON', the word*
*'TRAITOR' scrawled in red across the headshot.*
YVONNE *sees it.* MOLLY, *angry, upset, crumples it in a ball.*
*A trio of girls changing near by. Giggling, sneaking looks.* YVONNE
*turns on the trio. Bland faces.*
YVONNE: Who did that?
WHITWORTH: (*Strong English middle-class accent*) Who did
    what, Abelson?
YVONNE: (*Mimicking*) Who did what, Abelson?
WHITWORTH: Why doesn't your father come back, Molly? And
    take his punishment like a man.
MOLLY: You don't know what you're talking about.
WHITWORTH: Everyone knows he's a Communist traitor –
MOLLY: Oh, *voetsak* –
YVONNE: You weren't even born here –
    (*She advances on them with her lacrosse stick. A* TEACHER
    *appears, blowing a whistle, shouting at the girls to hurry.*)

## 33. EXT. ROTH PATIO/GARDENS. DAY
*The patio doors leading to the living room are wide open, the sound*
*of Chubby Checker's 'Let's Twist Again' fills the afternoon.*
MILIUS *is vacuuming the living room, twisting with the machine.*
MOLLY *and* YVONNE, *in school uniforms, twisting on the patio.*
*They're working on a routine, with hula hoops – turns, jumps,*
*complicated manoeuvres.* MIRIAM *is with them, trying to follow*
*them.*
YVONNE *takes a photograph of* MOLLY.
*At the foot of the driveway, two* AFRICAN MEN. *One older,*
*distinguished, dressed in an overcoat. The other smiling at them,*
*amused. The dog runs to them, barking. The track ends.*
YVONNE: Let's do it again.
MIRIAM: There's men over there.
    (*The dog barking furiously at the men. Other dogs in the*
    *vicinity, unseen, join in.*)

51

MOLLY, *followed by* MIRIAM, *runs across to them.* YVONNE
*– left hula-hooping on the patio.* MOLLY *hits the dog.*)
MOLLY: Shut up!
(*The younger man,* SOLOMON, *smiles at her.*)
SOLOMON: My name is Solomon Mabusa. This is Sipho
Dlamini. I'm Elsie's brother.
MOLLY: (*To* MIRIAM) Go and fetch her.
(MIRIAM *runs off.* MOLLY *holds on to the dog who growls
softly. She looks at* SOLOMON, *curious, taking him in, stares
at a brightly coloured beaded bracelet on his wrist.*)
Are you the one who's been in jail?
(*He laughs.*)
SOLOMON: Yes.
(*From the patio, 'Let's Twist Again' once more.* YVONNE *calls
out impatiently.*)
MOLLY: (*Shouting back*) I'm coming!
(YVONNE *twists on her own.*
ELSIE *comes running from the house, with* MIRIAM. *The dog
suddenly breaks free from* MOLLY*'s grasp, throws itself at*
SOLOMON *and* SIPHO, *barking furiously. Other dogs, unseen,
join in.* MOLLY, ELSIE *and* MIRIAM *shout and hit at the dog
who slinks off into a corner of the garden.* ELSIE *swears in her
own language at the dog.*)
SOLOMON: Is she here?
ELSIE: Yes.
SOLOMON: We need to see her.
MOLLY: I'll take you.
(SOLOMON *and* ELSIE *exchange a few words in their
vernacular, then the two men follow* MOLLY *to the house.*)

34. INT. CORRIDOR. DAY
SOLOMON *clicks his fingers, sings 'like we did last summer'.*
MOLLY *looks at him, shy, her eye caught again by his beaded
bracelet.* SOLOMON *holds out his wrist.*
SOLOMON: Black for the people. Green for the land. Yellow for
the gold.
(*The door to the study is closed.* MOLLY *knocks, the typing
stops.* DIANA *opens the door. She looks at* MOLLY, *then past
her, surprised, pleased.*)
Sorry we didn't phone –

52

DIANA: It's fine. Come in.
> (*She opens the door for them.* SOLOMON *turns, smiles his thanks at* MOLLY, *before the door is closed on her. She stands there for a moment, listening. What she hears:*)

SIPHO: (*Voice over*) We've decided to give you another contact.

DIANA: (*Voice over*) Will they get in touch with me in the usual way?

SIPHO: (*Voice over*) No. Something went wrong. We've changed the procedure –

YVONNE: (*Voice over*) Molly, man!
> (*She glares at* MOLLY *at the end of the corridor.*)

## 35. EXT. ROTH PATIO. NIGHT

*Diana's party. A multi-racial gathering, loud* kwela *music, talk, laughter emanating from the brightly lit house.*

*A few gathered on the patio: chatting, eating from plates balanced on their knees. A young black woman, slightly tipsy, dances on her own.*

YVONNE *and* MOLLY *come out from the house. They're in party dresses, too much make-up, hair teased and sprayed.* MOLLY *is trying to hide a bottle,* YVONNE *carries a couple of glasses.* MIRIAM, *in pyjamas and dressing gown, following them.* MOLLY *turns on her.*

MOLLY: Stop following us.

    (MIRIAM, *upset, turns to go back into the house.*)

## 36. INT. ROTH LIVING ROOM. NIGHT
*Laughter and talk through the loud music, the centre of the room packed with dancers. A black woman dancing on her own, brilliantly. Others, black and white, join in with her for a spell, then move away. She dances on, oblivious.*
*A white woman dancing with a black man, her movements jerky and self-conscious where his are fluid and confident.*
*A bearded academic type, alone in an armchair, clutching a drink, staring at the dance floor.* MIRIAM *and* JUDE, *in pyjamas, watching from the sofa.*
*A black man and a white woman kissing.* YVONNE *stares at them.*
MILIUS *is barman. He's tipsy, dancing behind the bar.* ELSIE *and a couple of other black women, in uniform, organizing food.*
DIANA *laughing in a group, including* SOLOMON.
MOLLY *and* YVONNE *with the combo of* MUSICIANS, MOLLY *requesting something. One of the musicians nods. Then the girls make their way through the dancers to* DIANA. HAROLD *is nearby.*

HAROLD: Hello, Molly. How's school?

MOLLY: (*Polite*) Fine, thanks. Mom, they're still up!

    (DIANA *looks across at* JUDE *and* MIRIAM. SOLOMON *smiles at* MOLLY; *she smiles back, shy.*)

DIANA: Try and see if you can get them to bed –

MOLLY: No. They won't listen to me. Anyway, they're going to play our song –

    (*The musicians stop what they're playing, to groans and protests from the dancers, then launch into 'Let's Twist Again'.*
    MOLLY *and* YVONNE *jump straight into their routine. There are cheers and whistles, and others join in.*)

## 37. EXT. ROTH DRIVEWAY. NIGHT
*Police cars pull into the driveway. A party guest runs into the house ahead of them.*

## 38. EXT. PATIO. NIGHT

*Two armed and uniformed policemen with dogs emerge from the
darkness and start herding those gathered on the patio towards the
living room. There are angry shouts and protests.*

## 39. INT. LIVING ROOM. NIGHT

*For a moment there is complete chaos and the one consistent thing is
the speed with which glasses are emptied into every available
receptacle as armed and uniformed police converge into the room.
The bird cage holding the yellow canary is flooded.*
*The supervising officer,* DETECTIVE KRUGER, *stands in the
doorway.*
*A police photographer stands on a table, photographing the guests.*
DIANA *steps forward, cool.*

DIANA: Can I see your warrant?
   (KRUGER *hands her a piece of paper.*)
KRUGER: This is a warrant for the arrest of Gus Roth.
   (DIANA *deliberately scrutinizes the piece of paper. She looks
   up.*)
DIANA: He's not here.
KRUGER: I'm surprised, Mrs Roth. You're having a party
   without him.
MOLLY: (*Loudly*) It's her birthday.
   (KRUGER *stares at her, turns back to* DIANA.)
KRUGER: Where is he, Mrs Roth?
DIANA: You know as well as I do.
KRUGER: You mean he's gone? Running scared?
DIANA: If you like.
KRUGER: We'll just take a look around. I don't need a warrant,
   Mrs Roth, to charge you under section 94 of the
   Prohibition of Intoxicating Liquor Act which prohibits the
   supply of alcoholic beverages to blacks.
DIANA: Do you see anyone here with a drink?
   (KRUGER *looks around. No one is holding a glass.*)
KRUGER: (*Raising his voice*) We want the names of everybody
   here.
   (*He barks out an order in Afrikaans to his men. A few take out
   notebooks, others leave the room.*
   YVONNE *looks scared.*)
YVONNE: (*To* MOLLY) Why does he want our names? Is he

55

going to take my name too?
MOLLY: No. We're not old enough.

40. INT. MOLLY'S ROOM. NIGHT
MOLLY *and* YVONNE *watch as a very young-looking policeman
searches the room.* DIANA *stands in the doorway, arms folded.
Molly hiccups.*
*The policeman opens the closet, gets down on his hands and knees.
The sight of his bum in the air is too much for* YVONNE. *She giggles
loudly.* MOLLY *looks panicked, hiccups loudly.*
*The policeman gets up, red-faced. He walks out of the room.*
DIANA: Go to bed, you two. (*She closes the door.*)
YVONNE: Doesn't he remind you of someone? Sideways.
MOLLY: No. Who?
YVONNE: Troy Donahue!
MOLLY: You're mad.

41. EXT. GARDEN. NIGHT
MOLLY *burns her secret file on Gus and Diana. Then she tramples
the ashes, scattering them.*

42. EXT. ROTH GARDEN. MORNING
MOLLY, JUDE *and* YVONNE *stand beneath a tree. They're wearing
formal school uniforms,* MOLLY's *different from the other two.*
JUDE *is on her knees, digging a shallow hole with a small spade.*
MIRIAM *is holding on to the dog who strains in the direction of the
dead canary* MOLLY *holds in a handkerchief. She folds the corners
to cover the bird and places it in the grave, covering it with dirt.*
*In the distance,* MILIUS *clearing the debris from the party.*
JUDE: We should say a prayer.
MOLLY: We're atheists, Jude. (*A pause.*) We could do what the
    Quakers do. Everyone stands in silence and then when you
    think of something to say then you say it.
    (*A pause.*)
MIRIAM: My favourite in the six times table is six times nine
    equals fifty-four –
MOLLY: It's supposed to be something about who you're
    burying. About the bird.
    (*A pause.*)
JUDE: Once it nearly died when the cage crashed to the floor.

56

*(Offscreen the sound of a car horn. A glimpse of a station-*
*wagon, other schoolgirls.* DIANA *at the patio doors, dressed in a*
*suit, a briefcase under one arm. She calls out to them.*
*As they run to the house the dog goes straight to the grave and*
*digs up the bird.)*


43. EXT. SCHOOL PLAYING FIELDS. DAY
*Girls in groups on the edge of the lacrosse pitch. The teacher blows*
*on a whistle and the first group sets off, cradling across the pitch.*
*The whistle blows again and a second group sets off,* MOLLY *and*
YVONNE *among them.*
*Two-thirds of the way across the pitch, obviously prearranged,*
MOLLY *and* YVONNE *cradle off away.*


44. INT. SCHOOL LAVATORIES. DAY
YVONNE: *Uno, dos, tres –*
     (YVONNE *and* MOLLY *fooling around with their castanets. It's*
     *uproar.*
     *The teacher walks in, red-faced, sweaty, shouting at them*
     *through the din.)*


45. INT. HEADMISTRESS'S OFFICE. DAY
MRS HARRIS: . . . do you have anything to say?
     (*A pause. The room densely forbidding, the shutters drawn*
     *against the sun.* MRS HARRIS, *the headmistress, sits behind a*
     *desk, talking through a cigarette. The air is thick with smoke.*
     YVONNE *and* MOLLY *stand in front of her, eyes lowered,*
     *hands clasped behind their backs.)*
     That's all, then.
     (*They curtsy, turn to leave.*)
     Molly. Stay behind.
     (YVONNE *leaves.* MRS HARRIS *lights a cigarette from the butt*
     *of the old ones.*)
     Is there anything you'd like to tell me?
     (MOLLY *looks at her, confused.*)
     (*Softer.*) Is everything all right at home?
MOLLY: Yes, ma'am.
MRS HARRIS: Have you heard from your father?
MOLLY: No, ma'am.

(*A long pause.*)
MRS HARRIS: All right, child. You may go.


46. INT. ROTH DINING ROOM. LATE AFTERNOON
DIANA *and the children eating supper.* BERTHA *is with them.*
MILIUS *serves.*
MIRIAM *slouches in her chair, feeds the dog.*
DIANA *leafs through a pile of papers, correcting proofs.*
BERTHA: (*To* MIRIAM) Stop that. You pick up all kinds of
diseases from animals.
MIRIAM: What diseases?
BERTHA: Leprosy, polio, scabies, rheumatism . . .
  (DIANA *looks at her, then back at her papers.*
  MOLLY *stuffs her mouth with food, chews, not swallowing.*
  *Off screen a car approaching, a door is slammed. Footsteps,*
  *then* HAROLD *comes into the room. He's agitated.*)
HAROLD: Diana, can we talk . . .
  (*She gets up. He follows her out of the room.*)
  We think we know who's been talking.
  (*He closes the door.*
  *Angle on* MOLLY. *Her mouth is full. She sneaks a look at*
  BERTHA, *then cups one hand around her mouth. She kicks*
  JUDE *under the table,* JUDE *starts and looks at her.* MOLLY
  *opens her mouth wide. Jude's POV is a mouthful of chewed*
  *food. She screams.* MOLLY *splutters, sends food around the*
  *table.* MIRIAM *thinks it's hilarious.*)
BERTHA: You're very immature at times, child.
  (MIRIAM *stuffs her mouth with food, opens it wide, at*
  MOLLY, JUDE, BERTHA. BERTHA *suddenly clips her over the*
  *head, not hard, but enough of a rebuke.* MIRIAM *starts to cry.*
  MOLLY *gets up from the table, walks out of the room.*)


47. EXT. ROTH DRIVEWAY. LATE AFTERNOON
MOLLY *stands in the doorway, watching* HAROLD *and* DIANA
*talking by his car. After a moment he gets in and reverses down the*
*driveway.* DIANA *walks back towards the house, preoccupied,*
*frowning.*
MOLLY: (*Tentative*) Who was it, Mom, who?
DIANA: Who was what, Molly?
MOLLY: Who's been talking?

DIANA: Nobody.

MOLLY: What was Harold talking about?

DIANA: Nothing.

(MOLLY *moves away from the doorway to let* DIANA *past.*)

MOLLY: The headmistress asked me questions today. About Daddy.

(DIANA *turns around to look at her.*)

DIANA: What questions?

(*No reply.*)

What did she say?

MOLLY: Nothing.

(*She walks away.*)


48. INT. MOLLY'S ROOM. NIGHT

MOLLY *suddenly awake, disturbed by sounds off screen. She starts out of bed.*


49. EXT. DRIVEWAY. NIGHT

DIANA *walks quickly down the driveway. A car waits at the bottom, its headlights guiding her way.*

MOLLY *comes running out of the house towards her.*

MOLLY: (*Terrified*) Mom!!

(DIANA *turns, startled.*)

Where are you going?

DIANA: To the township. There's a bus protest.

MOLLY: (*Quickly*) Can I come?

DIANA: It's five thirty in the morning. You've got school –

MOLLY: Oh, please. Let me come with. Please.

(DIANA *reflects for a moment.*)

DIANA: OK. Go and put on your uniform. Hurry.

(MOLLY *dashes back into the house.*)


50. EXT. RAILWAY LINES. DAWN

*Black workers cross the railway line. A couple of locomotives shunt coal wagons.*


51. EXT. CITY STREET. TELEGRAPH ROAD. DAWN

*Day breaks as Harold's car drives towards the township.* DIANA *beside him,* MOLLY *in the back in her school uniform, her satchel beside her.*

## 52. EXT. TOWNSHIP. MORNING

HAROLD *drives slowly past scores of black workers, marching towards the city. Men and women, many balancing heavy loads on their heads. The mood is cheerful and defiant.*

DIANA *talks into a tape recorder.*

DIANA: The mood is cheerful, defiant, singing, chanting 'Azikhwelwa' – They shall not be ridden . . . 'Asinamali' – We have no money . . . Over the rise that obscures Alexandra Township from the main road comes an eruption of workers in the dawn hours . . . End to end the road is filled with shadowy, hurrying figures . . . Men and women, old and young, many balancing heavy loads on their heads, babies tied securely to their backs . . .

*(HAROLD stops at the corner of an intersection. He gets out of the car with a camera, photographs the passing crowd.)*

HAROLD: There's Solomon.

*(In the distance, approaching the intersection, SOLOMON in the crowd, leading the singing. He sees them, walks over.)*

SOLOMON: Come and join us. We need a few white faces . . .

*(He sees MOLLY in the back.)*

Hey, my little twisting sister. Are you marching with us?

MOLLY: I can't. I've got to go to school.

SOLOMON: Shame. Well, I'm glad to see you.

*(He rejoins the marchers. HAROLD drives off slowly. A group of young Africans, a young girl with them, approach the car. They encircle it, smiling in at the windows, thump the roof, one on the bonnet. High-spirited, not unfriendly.)*

YOUTHS: Hey, give us a ride . . . Come on, please . . . It's a long walk . . .

*(HAROLD stops and they crowd into the back with MOLLY. They're exuberant and friendly, and she's thrilled as they exchange greetings and friendly insults with others in the crowd. Police along the route. Stopping men and women at random, demanding pass books, searching through belongings. A POLICEMAN steps out into the road and directs HAROLD to pull over. He signals for reinforcements, stares at DIANA and HAROLD, at MOLLY and the youths crowded together in the back.)*

POLICEMAN: *(To YOUTHS, in Afrikaans)* Get out!

DIANA: Wait a minute. Is it against the law to give them a ride?

(*The* POLICEMAN *stares at her. A* SECOND POLICEMAN, *more senior, steps forward.*)

SECOND POLICEMAN: Do you have a licence?

DIANA: A licence for what?

SECOND POLICEMAN: For carrying passengers.

DIANA: We're reporters, not taxi drivers.

SECOND POLICEMAN: Don't get smart with me. (*To the youths*) Get out of there!

(*He draws his gun, levels it straight at them. In silence, the youths get out of the car. The* SECOND POLICEMAN *stares at* MOLLY.)

Who's this?

DIANA: My daughter.

SECOND POLICEMAN: *Sies*. Next thing she'll be sleeping with the kaffirs.

DIANA: Judging from the coloured population your forefathers didn't do too badly.

(HAROLD *laughs*.)

## 53. EXT. ABELSON HOUSE. NIGHT

*The house is expansive, set in acres of landscaped garden. There's a large marquee; tables scattered around the patio are by the swimming pool, clusters of Chinese lanterns hanging from the trees.*

*Silent gliding African men servants, in formal waiting gear with white gloves, dispensing drinks and snacks from silver trays.*

*A combo on an elevated platform. Guests cha cha cha.*

*The women wear thick make-up and stiffly sprayed bouffant hairdos. The men are all in suits. There's a lot of circulating, hearty laughter, lavish greeting.*

MOLLY *at a table with* YVONNE *and a couple of slightly older* BOYS.

YVONNE: Boy! Boy! Come here!

(*A waiter near by, holding a tray of drinks.*)

MOLLY: I bet you his name isn't boy –

YVONNE: Oh, shut up. He's just helping. I don't know what his name is.

MOLLY: Anyway, he's a man!

(JUNE ABELSON *plonks herself down on* YVONNE'*s lap. She's very animated, slightly tipsy.*)

JUNE: Hello, darlings. Are you having a fabulous time?

61

(*She reaches across the table to grab* MOLLY's *face as* YVONNE *squirms uncomfortably.*)
You look so serious, Molly. Relax. Enjoy yourself. Dance, circulate . . .

YVONNE: Mom. My dress, man!
(JUNE *grabs her daughter, gives her a huge kiss, leaves a lipstick smear all over her face.*)

JUNE: God. You're so gorgeous. Look at this face! Will you look at this face! I could eat it up . . .

YVONNE: Mom. Get *off* me.
(JUNE *laughs, leaves.* YVONNE *turns to one of the* BOYS.)
Let's dance. (*Rubbing her cheek*) Is there lipstick?
(MOLLY *and the second* BOY *sit a while in silence, looking everywhere but at each other.* MOLLY *slurps at her drink through a straw.*)

## 54. INT. MARQUEE. NIGHT

MOLLY *wanders through to the buffet table. An abundance of food. Nearby a* WOMAN *helping herself, talking all the while to* SECOND WOMAN, *in full hearing of the African waiters.*

FIRST WOMAN: She's giving me so much trouble. She's got so many problems and her husband's in jail. She's got sixty

cousins, twenty aunties, and they all live off me. I'm always
saying, Sara, where's the sugar? Why is there never sugar?
SECOND WOMAN: (*Laughing*) For Christ's sake, Karen, get rid
of her. I can ask my girl if she knows anybody.
FIRST WOMAN: I mean, I sympathize with her. She's a good
girl, she's very clean. (*Laughs.*) She can have the sugar but
every month there's a bloody funeral or – a bloody –
(*Pointing, to one of the waiters*) – I'll take some more of the
salmon.
(MOLLY *stares at the* WOMEN, *walks away.*)

55. INT. ABELSON HOUSE. JUNE'S BEDROOM. NIGHT
*The door is open. The bed is piled with coats.* MOLLY *walks in.*
*What she sees:* JUNE, *bent over the toilet in the en suite bathroom.*
MOLLY *backs quietly away.*

56. EXT. ABELSON PATIO. NIGHT
GERALD ABELSON, *meticulous, immaculately dressed, in a huddle*
*of men.* MOLLY *hovers.*
GERALD: Do you want something, Molly?
MOLLY: Have you seen Yvonne?
GERALD: No. Yes. (*Points vaguely.*) Over there.
   (MOLLY *walks off.* GERALD *looks after her and says*
   *something to the group of men. They turn to stare at her.*)

57. INT. ABELSON KITCHEN. NIGHT
*Every available surface is covered with food and glasses. The*
*waiters deposit empty plates. Three African women wash up,*
*prepare platters, dry glasses. They are talking and laughing together*
*in their own language.*
*One woman,* PEGGY, *smiles at* MOLLY.
PEGGY: Come in. Here. Sit here. Out of the way. Have you
eaten? Have you tried my blintzes?
   (*She says something to the other women. They exclaim, stop*
   *working to look curiously at* MOLLY. *They smile at her.*)
They are brave people, your mother and father. You must
be proud of them.
   (MOLLY *embarrassed, pleased.*
   JUNE *walks in, stares at a tray of hors d'oeuvres a waiter has*
   *picked up to take out.*)

63

JUNE: No, Peggy, what's the matter with you, man? Not
enough olives. And where's the parsley? And the colour:
where's the red pepper? (*To* MOLLY) Hello, darling.
(*She kisses her on the cheek, then lifts a tray, sails out of the
kitchen.*)
Come on, chop-chop. People are starving out there.

58. EXT. ABELSON DRIVEWAY. MORNING
MOLLY *comes running out of the house, carrying an overnight bag.*
DIANA *is waiting in her car.* JUNE *leans on the door, talking to her
through the open window. She's in her dressing gown, dark glasses,
hung over.*
MOLLY: Thanks, June.
(*She gets into the car.*)
DIANA: How was the party?
JUNE: (*Playfully*) You didn't invite me to yours so I didn't
invite you to mine. (*She giggles.*) You would've hated the
crowd. Gerald's friends, mostly. Still, it was fun! That's
why my parties work – I *always* have a good time. (*She
laughs, then, serious.*) Diana, seriously, if there's anything I
can do to help.
(DIANA *looks at her. She has no idea what she's talking
about.*)
It's not that I'm not busy. But I could make time. I mean I
can answer the phone or something and I was a typist in
my time . . .
DIANA: (*Smiling at* JUNE) Thanks, June.
(*She looks past her to where* GERALD *stands, in dressing gown
and hair-net, in the doorway of the house. He waves stiffly,
forces a smile. He's clearly terrified of her.*)

59. INT. DIANA'S NEWSPAPER OFFICE BUILDING. DAY
DIANA *and* MOLLY *walk the flights of stairs to the top office.*
MOLLY *is dragging her feet.*
MOLLY: Mom. But it's Sunday.
DIANA: I'm just picking something up.
MOLLY: . . . so anyway, I think she's a secret drinker. I saw her
vomiting.
(DIANA *unlocks the door.*)
Yvonne says they're probably going to get a divorce. She

can't decide which one to stay with. It might be fun with
her dad because he's away on business all the time . . .
(*She stops, stares after* DIANA *at the office.*)

60. INT. DIANA'S NEWSPAPER OFFICE. DAY
*The room has been systematically ransacked and wrecked. Posters
and photographs are slashed, drawers upturned, papers everywhere,
red paint on the walls and floor. The Xerox machine and radio
smashed.*
MOLLY *watches as* DIANA *walks around in disbelief, picking at
some of the shredded papers strewn around her desk.* MOLLY *bends
to pick stuff up then starts, scared, as* DIANA *kicks out at an
overturned filing cabinet.*
DIANA *looks at* MOLLY.
DIANA: Let's go home.

61. INT. ASSEMBLY HALL. AFTERNOON
*An African man mops the floor, silently, methodically. At the other
end of the room, watched over by a bored* PREFECT, MOLLY *and*
YVONNE *wipe and dust the arrangement of school photographs –
groupings of sports teams, past heads, eminent past pupils – all
women, all white.*
*Off screen the sound of a team game in the distance, the faint
tinkling of pianos being practised.*
*They dust in silence.* YVONNE *sneaks a look at the* PREFECT,
*mouths something to* MOLLY. MOLLY *doesn't get it. The* PREFECT
*yawns, turns to stare out of the window.* YVONNE *nudges* MOLLY,
*turns to face the* PREFECT, *pulls a hideous face and gestures wildly
at her.* MOLLY *looks away from her, trying to keep from laughing.*
YVONNE *nudges her again then quickly lifts her dress above her
head, wiggling her body.* MOLLY *snorts out loud, the* PREFECT
*whips around.*
PREFECT: It doesn't worry me how long you take. I've got all
afternoon.
(MOLLY *looks over at the African man. He's leaning against
the mop, lost in reverie.*)

62. EXT. SCHOOL. AFTERNOON
*Girls pour out of the school to waiting transport.* MOLLY *and*
YVONNE *among them.*
BERTHA *stands by her car.* JUDE *sits in the back.* MIRIAM *in front,*

*the top of her head barely visible above the seat.*
MOLLY: (*To* YVONNE) I'll see you tomorrow.
YVONNE: Don't forget your costume.
    (MOLLY, *surprised to see* BERTHA.)
MOLLY: Where's Mum?
BERTHA: She's at home. She asked me to pick you up.
MOLLY: But we're supposed to get the lace. She promised!
BERTHA: She didn't say anything to me.
    (MOLLY *walks angrily to the front passenger seat, stares in at*
    MIRIAM *through the window.* MIRIAM *tries to disappear into*
    *the seat.* MOLLY *stands there, staring at her.* MIRIAM, *furious,*
    *climbs over the front seat into the back.* MOLLY *takes her place*
    *in the front.*)

63. INT. BERTHA'S CAR. AFTERNOON
*In the back,* JUDE *has an open book pulled up to her face.*
JUDE: OK. Give me the facts about Sir Francis Drake.
MIRIAM: Don't know.
JUDE: You do. What was he like before he was a pirate?
MIRIAM: Don't know.
JUDE: (*Exasperated*) It says here he was a reliable and
    dependable man –
MIRIAM: I *hate* that kind of man!
    (MIRIAM *kicks out at the seat in front of her.* MOLLY *whirls*
    *around to face her.*)
MOLLY: Don't do that.
MIRIAM: I didn't do anything!
MOLLY: You kicked me.
BERTHA: Please, children.
MOLLY: Gran, I have to get the lace for my costume. The
    competition's on Monday.
BERTHA: You must ask your mother.
MOLLY: She's too busy all the time. (*Whirling around in her seat*)
    Stop kicking me! Stop doing that! You're doing it on
    purpose –
    (BERTHA *pulls into the side, stops the car.*)

64. EXT. BERTHA'S CAR. AFTERNOON
MOLLY *gets out of the car and into the back as* MIRIAM *clambers*
*over the seat to the front.* BERTHA *pulls away.*

66

65. EXT. ROTH DRIVEWAY. AFTERNOON
*Bertha's car pulls into the driveway. There are two large cars parked
at the head, near the entrance to the house.*
BERTHA *parks. A man in a suit walks out of the house, carrying an
armful of papers. The children run ahead, stop in the doorway.*
BERTHA *comes up behind them.*


66. INT. ROTH LIVING ROOM. AFTERNOON
BERTHA: Oh, my God.
> (*What they see: the room is in total disarray, the result of a
> thorough and brutal search. Drawers and filing cabinets have
> been emptied out, books pulled from the shelves, thrown
> randomly on the floor. Cushions ripped open, feathers
> everywhere.*
> *Plainclothes and uniformed policemen sift through the chaos,
> consult among themselves.*
> ELSIE *and* MILIUS *hovering, scared. The children follow*
> BERTHA *through the living room and into the study.*)


67. INT. STUDY. AFTERNOON
DIANA *is with* KRUGER *in the study, watching as he sifts through
papers on the desk. She looks shaken, scared. Another policeman has
his arms piled high with papers and books.* DIANA *grabs at a book
near the top of the pile.*
DIANA: You're not going to take the address book. You can't
    take that! It's got the telephone numbers of our doctor, our
    dentist, our butcher. And all the children's friends –
KRUGER: There are names and numbers of banned people in
    there.
DIANA: For God's sake, I'm a reporter.
> (*She looks across, sees* BERTHA *and the children.*)
They're arresting me.
BERTHA: No.
DIANA: It's ninety days.
BERTHA: Oh, God.
DIANA: Mom, please . . .
> (MOLLY *staring at the desk, the secret drawer undiscovered.*)
KRUGER: Go and pack your suitcase, Mrs Roth.
> (*She looks at him, walks over to the children.*)
DIANA: Come with me. Come and help me.

### 68. INT. LIVING ROOM. AFTERNOON

DIANA *leads the children through the living room. At the door they have to stand aside to let a policeman pass, his arms loaded with books and a typewriter.*

MOLLY *steps out in front of him.*

MOLLY: That's my typewriter. Anyway, it's broken.

> (*The* POLICEMAN *ignores her.*)

> Hey . . .

DIANA: Don't bother. They'll take what they want.


### 69. INT. DIANA'S BEDROOM. AFTERNOON

*A* POLICEMAN *watches as* DIANA *takes things from the wardrobe and drawers, placing them in an open suitcase on the bed. She's moving automatically. She's afraid, and in shock, and trying not to show this to the children.*

DIANA: Jude, don't forget to remind Gran about the
orthodontist this week. Molly, you must ask the Abelsons
to collect you for riding –

POLICEMAN: No books. Except the Bible. No paper. No
writing materials.

> (DIANA *stops, stares at him. She puts the notebook back on the dressing table.*)

MIRIAM: How long is ninety days?
JUDE: Three months. Twelve weeks. Ninety days.
MIRIAM: But, Mommy, it's my birthday . . .
  (*She starts to cry.* DIANA *bends, hugs her.*)
DIANA: Darling, your birthday's not until December. Of course
  I won't miss it. Darling, don't cry . . .
  (JUDE *is crying.* DIANA *reaches out to comfort her, blinking
  away her own tears.*
  BERTHA *appears in the doorway, behind* MOLLY. *She puts an
  arm around her, leans on her heavily.* MOLLY *pulls away and
  runs out of the room.*)

70. EXT. GARDEN. LATE AFTERNOON
MOLLY *stops in a corner of the garden. She cries, noisily and
unrestrainedly.* DIANA *has followed her out into the garden. She
takes* MOLLY *in her arms. She can't keep back her own tears. They
hug each other, then* MOLLY, *through her tears, sees the figure of*
KRUGER *right behind them.*
KRUGER: Let's go.
  (DIANA *gently disengages herself.* MOLLY *watches as she
  leaves with* KRUGER.)

69

### 71. INT. PRISON CORRIDOR. NIGHT

DIANA, *wearing the clothes she was arrested in, led by a wardress through the prison corridor. The sounds of doors being locked and  unlocked, echoing footsteps, voices shouting orders.*

### 72. INT. ROTH HOUSE. NIGHT

MOLLY, *half asleep, walking down the corridor.*

### 73. INT. DIANA'S ROOM. NIGHT

MOLLY *walks into the room. A figure asleep on the bed.*
MOLLY: Mom?
> (*The figure stirs, turns, flings an arm out.* MOLLY *stares at* BERTHA *asleep, the slack skin on her arm, her open mouth.*)

### 74. INT. CELL. DAY

DIANA *scratches a mark with a hairpin on the wall of the cell. Day nine. Nearby graffiti: 'I am here for murdering my baby. I am fourteen years old.' 'Magda loves Vincent Forever.' The hairpin breaks.*
*She drags the chair across to the window, wraps her hands in*

*Kleenex, pulls herself up to see out through the bars, standing on*
*tiptoe.*
*What she sees:*

75. EXT. MIDTOWN STREET. DAY
*A busy midtown street. The lunch hour: groups of office workers*
*entering restaurants. An African newsvendor on the corner directly*
*opposite. A section of his poster visible:*

*QUA*

*I*

*RHO*

76. INT. CELL. DAY
DIANA *strains to read.*
DIANA: (*Aloud, soft*) Rhodesia . . . Quarrel in . . . Rhodesia?
    . . . Qualms in . . . Rhodesia? . . . Quads? . . .

77. INT. ROTH DINING ROOM. DAY
BERTHA, JUDE *and* MIRIAM *at breakfast.* BERTHA *reading the*
*newspaper, the headline clearly visible:*

*QUAKE IN RHODESIA*

MOLLY *comes in, still wearing her mother's dressing gown.* JUDE
*and* MIRIAM *are in their school uniforms.*
BERTHA: When are you going back to school? Sooner or later
    you're going to have to –
MOLLY: That's Mom's seat.
    (BERTHA *looks at her, gets up, moves her setting and breakfast*
    *to another seat.*)
    That's where Dad sits.
    (*A pause.*)
BERTHA: Sometimes I wonder if you've got a heart.

78. INT. SCHOOL CORRIDORS. DAY
MOLLY *walks through the throng of girls. She quickens her pace, not*
*looking at them, as she passes* WHITWORTH *and her gang. They*
*stare after her curiously.*
YVONNE *is at her locker, with another girl,* DEBBIE. *They're deep*
*in conversation.*

MOLLY: Hello.
(YVONNE *is surprised to see her. And pleased. She smiles.*)
YVONNE: I didn't know when you were coming back.
MOLLY: You didn't try very hard to find out.
YVONNE: I was so busy, Molly. I had to get another
    partner . . .
MOLLY: I'm sorry about the competition.
YVONNE: Oh, it doesn't matter. It was stupid anyway. (*A
    pause.*) How's . . . Is your mother all right?
    (MOLLY *looks away. She doesn't know what to say.*)
    Have you seen her?
MOLLY: No. She's not allowed visitors yet.
    (*She looks very upset, on the verge of tears. An uncomfortable
    pause.* YVONNE *doesn't know what to say.* DEBBIE *stares at*
    MOLLY.)

79. INT. HEADMISTRESS'S OFFICE. DAY
MOLLY *on the edge of her chair, stiff.* MRS HARRIS, *wreathed in
cigarette smoke.*
MRS HARRIS: Do you need help in catching up with the work
    you've missed?
MOLLY: No. It's OK.
    (*A pause.*)
MRS HARRIS: How's your grandmother?
MOLLY: She's fine.
    (*A pause.*)
MRS HARRIS: She's not a young woman . . . (*A pause.*) If you
    find it difficult at home, you could come and board here.
    Just until . . . this is over.
    (MOLLY *is surprised.*)
    And if you want to talk. About anything. I'm here.
    (*A pause. Softer*) Have you visited your mother?
    (MOLLY *shakes her head. Again on the verge of tears.*)

80. INT. CLASSROOM. DAY
*A* TEACHER *stands at the blackboard, marking an early map of the
country with crosses.* THE BOER WAR, 1899–1901 *is heavily
underscored.*
TEACHER: . . . here is where women and children were kept in
    concentration camps by the British . . . (*She turns to face*

*the class.*) Like the American War of Independence, this was the Afrikaaner's fight for the liberty and independence of his country, our country.
(*She looks around, eyes resting on* MOLLY *who is staring out of the window.*)
Molly. Are you with us?
(MOLLY *starts.*)
GIRL: (*Loud whisper*) No – she's against us.
(*Titters.* MOLLY *blushes.*)


81. INT. PRISON ELEVATOR. DAY
DIANA, *accompanied by a wardress and a uniformed policeman.*

82. INT. PRISON INTERROGATION ROOM. DAY
*A desk, a few hardback chairs, barred windows.* DIANA, *composed, made up, facing the senior interrogating officer,* MULLER. *He's in his early forties, polite, soft-spoken. A second officer,* LE ROUX, *younger, taut, nervy, stands against a wall.*
DIANA *stares at a single paper clip on the floor. She covers it with a foot, drags it nearer.*
LE ROUX: You have nothing to say?
DIANA: Yes.
LE ROUX: Yes?
DIANA: I want to write to my children. I need pen and paper, please.
MULLER: Answer our questions. Sign a statement. In no time you'll be back with your children.
LE ROUX: Everyone else is talking. No one else will ever know.
(DIANA *bends quickly, picks up the paper clip.* MULLER *watches as she fiddles with it.* LE ROUX *stares at her, hard.*)
MULLER: We know all about you, anyway. We know you were a member of the Black Hand Secret Society –
(DIANA *laughs.*)
DIANA: What, for heaven's sake, is the 'Black Hand Secret Society'?
(MULLER *leans across the table with a series of black and white blow-ups. He holds them up to her, showing them to her one by one.*)
MULLER: This was on the fifth of May . . . This the eleventh . . . this, the twenty-seventh . . . This the fourteenth

June . . .
(*The photographs, taken from different angles and on different occasions, show* DIANA *entering the midtown apartment building in scene 21.*)

LE ROUX: The one who got away. You're lucky you were late.
(*On* DIANA. *Whatever she's feeling, she doesn't show.*)

DIANA: If you know so much, then why don't you charge me?
(*A pause.*)

LE ROUX: You're an obstinate woman, Mrs Roth. You're lucky we're decent people. We have feeling for women in this country.

83. INT. CELL. DAY
*As the door is closed and locked behind her,* DIANA *exhales deeply. For a moment we see the strain of the preceding interrogation, and the beginnings of a new vulnerability, even fear.*

84. INT. ELSIE'S ROOM. NIGHT
MOLLY *with* ELSIE, *looking through a photograph album. The photos are of Elsie's family, and her children, ranging in age from four to ten. They pose formally in front of a small house, one in a shanty-town settlement in a barren rural area.*

MOLLY: This is Nelson. Walter. Albertina. Lillian.

ELSIE: No. *This* is Lillian. The little one is Albertina.
(*A pause.* MOLLY *watching* ELSIE *looking at the photographs of her children.*)

MOLLY: Are you sad?

ELSIE: Yes. I am sad.

85. INT. CELL. DAY
DIANA *makes a mark on the wall. Day twenty-three. She rips at the thread of the hem on a dress, then folds it back and starts hemming it together again. Off screen heavy footsteps, getting nearer . . .*
DIANA *pauses, waits expectantly . . . the footsteps pass on by. She turns back to her sewing.*

86. EXT. PRISON YARD. DAY
*A small rectangle, fenced in by tall concrete and wire. A* WARDRESS *sits in a chair to one side.* DIANA *in a corner, on the ground, mesmerized by the movement of a bug. She draws her knees*

*up to her chin, turns her face to the sun's rays. A low-flying military*
*helicopter fills the sky, blocks the light for a moment.*

87. INT. PRISON CORRIDOR. DAY
DIANA *led through the corridor back to her cell by the* WARDRESS.
*They pause for a security door to be unlocked.*
WOMAN'S VOICE: Diana!
(DIANA *starts in recognition, turns to see* SAEEDA *at the other
end of the corridor. They wave at each other frantically.*)
Maria's here . . . and Thendi . . .
WARDRESS: You're not allowed to speak! I'll report you –
(*She tries to bustle* DIANA *away.*)
DIANA: (*Shouting back*) Are you all right?
WARDRESS: I'll report you!
DIANA: What'll you do to us? Put us in solitary?
(*Off screen* SAEEDA *laughing.*)

88. EXT. SCHOOL. DAY
MOLLY *emerges from the school with* YVONNE *and* DEBBIE.
YVONNE: . . . so we didn't get home until ten o'clock and my
dad went crazy. I'm not allowed out for the next two
weekends.
DEBBIE: I got home at eleven. My dad doesn't even care.
(MOLLY, *listening, left out.*
*A woman shouts from her car, toots her horn.* DEBBIE *waves at
her.*)
There's my mom –
MOLLY: (*To* YVONNE) I'll come home with you. I'll get my gran
to pick me up –
DEBBIE: Are you coming? My mom's got to go . . .
(YVONNE *uncomfortable,* DEBBIE *tugging at her arm.*)
YVONNE: (*To* MOLLY) Look, I'll phone you.
(*She runs off with* DEBBIE. MOLLY *turns away, stung. As*
YVONNE *gets into Debbie's mother's car, she watches, torn, as*
MOLLY *crosses the road.*)

89. EXT. PORCH. DAY
MOLLY *sits on the steps, her knees drawn up, sucking her thumb.*

90. INT. LIVING ROOM. DAY
MOLLY *plays the piano, a waltz. She turns her head, smiles. What*

*she sees: Flashcut.* GUS *and* DIANA, *waltzing together in the low afternoon light.*

91. INT. DINING ROOM. LATE AFTERNOON
MOLLY *wanders in, then stops as she sees* MILIUS *bent over the drinks cabinet. He has his back to her. She watches as he drinks straight from a bottle. He wipes the top, studies the level, replaces it, walks out of the room.*
MOLLY *picks up the telephone, dials. Behind her,* ELSIE *comes in, quietly lays the table.*
MOLLY: Hello? This is Molly. (*Listens.*) I'm fine thank you. Is Yvonne there? (*Listens.*) Oh. OK. Goodbye.
  (*She puts the phone down.* ELSIE *watches as she walks out of the room.*)

92. INT. ABELSON LIVING ROOM. LATE AFTERNOON
JUNE *is fixing herself a drink. She looks out of the window.*

93. EXT. ABELSON POOL. LATE AFTERNOON
YVONNE, *with* DEBBIE *and the two boys from the party playing in the pool.*

94. INT. MOLLY'S ROOM. LATE AFTERNOON
MIRIAM *is dressing up in the Spanish dancing dress.* JUDE *lies across Molly's bed, reading a comic.*
MOLLY *comes in, thundery.*
MOLLY: Take that off.
MIRIAM: Oh, Molly –
MOLLY: Get out of my room.
  (*She starts to pull the dress off* MIRIAM *who is in tears.* JUDE *hides behind her comic.*)
  (*To* JUDE) And you.
JUDE: What did I do?
MOLLY: Get out.
  (JUDE *and* MIRIAM *leave.* MOLLY *puts the dress back on its hanger, stares at it for a moment, then grabs a sweater and climbs out of the window.*)

95. EXT. ABELSON HOUSE, STREET. LATE AFTERNOON
MOLLY, *hot and grubby, runs across the street, then alongside a*

*fence of thick shrubbery. She stops, parts the hedge. What she sees:*

96. EXT. ABELSON GARDEN, POOL. LATE AFTERNOON
YVONNE, DEBBIE *and the two boys in the pool, laughing, fooling around.*

97. EXT. ABELSON HOUSE, GATE ENTRANCE. LATE
AFTERNOON
*High, double, barred gates.* MOLLY *presses the intercom. She waits. Off screen the sound of laughter from the pool. She presses again, longer. Dogs bark from inside the grounds.*
AFRICAN VOICE: (*Loud, static*) Yes?
MOLLY: (*Stuttering*) It's Molly. I want to see Yvonne.
    (*More static.*)
AFRICAN VOICE: Who is it? Who?
MOLLY: (*Louder*) Is Yvonne there? It's me, Molly . . .
    (*Sudden silence. Then the buzzer sounds, and the gates click ajar.* MOLLY *opens a gate as* JUNE *walks hurriedly from the house towards her.*
    *A car swings into the driveway from the street, headlights full on, horn staccato.*
    GERALD *gets out of the car. The engine is still running. He peers through the twilight at her.* JUNE *has reached the gates.*)
GERALD: Who's that? Molly?
MOLLY: I want to see Yvonne –
GERALD: Who brought you here?
MOLLY: Nobody.
GERALD: Then how did you get here?
MOLLY: I walked.
JUNE: You walked? Don't you know how dangerous it is –
    (GERALD *crosses to the passenger side of the car and opens the door.*)
GERALD: Get in. I'm taking you home.
MOLLY: But I want to see Yvonne –
GERALD: Get in.
JUNE: Gerald, let me take her –
GERALD: Get in the car!
    (MOLLY *runs off away from him.* GERALD *gets into the car, angrily reverses into the street.*)

**98. EXT. STREET. LATE AFTERNOON**
GERALD *slows as he approaches* MOLLY *running along the*
*pavement. He stops, gets out of the car, runs after her, grabs her by*
*the wrists and drags her over to the passenger seat.*

**99. EXT. ROTH DRIVEWAY. DUSK**
MOLLY *shoots out of Gerald's car, races up the driveway.* BERTHA
*and* ELSIE *come out of the house,* JUDE *and* MIRIAM *with them.*
BERTHA: You gave us such a terrible fright . . .
    (MOLLY *runs past her to* ELSIE. ELSIE *takes her in her arms,*
    *rocking her, calming her.*)

**100. INT. PRISON INTERROGATION ROOM. DAY**
DIANA, *facing* MULLER *and another plainclothes policeman, angry-*
*looking, snapping gum.* MULLER, *inscrutable.* DIANA *rubbing at her*
*temples. Paler. Thinner.*
MULLER: (*Gently*) You don't look too good.
DIANA: My ulcer's playing up. I'm having difficulty sleeping.
MULLER: I'll arrange for you to see the doctor.
    (*He gathers together the files and notebooks on the desk, starts to*
    *put them back in his briefcase. He sees something, smiles, hands a*

*sheet of paper to* DIANA.)
My son did it.
(*It's a drawing of a fish.* DIANA *laughs.*)

DIANA: He's given them noses!
(*They both laugh. The policeman stares at them.*)
How old is he?

MULLER: He's six. (*A pause.*) Three months older than Miriam.
(*On* DIANA *for a beat. Then* MULLER *stands, picks up his briefcase. The policeman walks out of the room. A wardress comes in, stands by for* DIANA.)

DIANA: (*Light, strained*) Is that it then?
(MULLER *looks at her, walks out of the room. She stares after him. Abandoned.*)

## IOI. EXT. TOWNSHIP STREETS. DAY

*An old and battered taxi drives slowly through the unpaved dusty streets, dodging burning garbage, past rows of corrugated housing, makeshift shacks, open lots.*

*The driver is black.* ELSIE *and* MOLLY *in the back. A long line to a single water tap. Gallon drums and other containers balanced on women's and children's heads.*

*Past a shebeen – loud* kwela *music, laughter, a group of men gathered*

*outside, one passed out on the street. The taxi pulls up outside an all-purpose grocery store.* ELSIE *pays the driver.*

## 102. EXT. GROCERY STORE/TOWNSHIP STREETS. DAY
MOLLY *waits as* ELSIE *goes into the store.*
*Near by a group of old people on chairs outside their homes. An old woman has a young child spread across her lap as she sews a patch on to the back of his trousers.*
*Children play in the street with balls and makeshift toys: hoops and sticks, rubber tyres, dustbin lids, homemade carts, in wrecked and burnt cars. They stare at* MOLLY: *curious, shy, not unfriendly.*
ELSIE *comes out with an iced Coke.* MOLLY *drinks thirstily as they set off down the street.*

## 103. EXT. SOLOMON'S HOUSE. DAY
ELSIE *leads* MOLLY *through the gate, past scrawny chickens scrabbling in the dust. A child stares at* MOLLY, *runs into the house. Three youths, sharp, proud, come out from the house. They walk past* MOLLY *and* ELSIE, *greet* ELSIE. MOLLY *stops, stares at them, at one in particular, caught by his stature. His look passes over her.*
SOLOMON *stands in the doorway, smiling.*

104. INT. SOLOMON'S HOUSE. DAY
*Dim, clean, sparse. A large table virtually fills the main room. Around it are a very old man, a few women, about six children of various ages.*
SOLOMON: Welcome to my house. (*Sings, twisting*)

> 'Let's twist again
> Like we did last summer . . .'

(*He smiles at* MOLLY.)
She is the champion twister, this one.
(*Everyone in the room looking at her curiously, shyly, not unwelcoming.* MOLLY *moves closer to* ELSIE, *uncertain.* SOLOMON *puts an arm around one of the women.*)
This is my wife. And these are my children.
(*He pulls out three of the youngest children.* MOLLY *smiles at a little girl.*)
MOLLY: What's your name?
(*The child is overcome by shyness. She bursts out laughing, her hand up to her mouth. The other children laugh. For a moment* MOLLY *is confused, then can't help but laugh with them. She*

*turns to another of Solomon's children.*)
What's your name?
(*They're off again.*)
SOLOMON: Come, sit down. You must eat in my house.
(*He propels her to a chair, vacated by one of the women, next to the old man. He turns as she sits, stares at her with clouded eyes.*)
ELSIE: This is our grandfather. He is blind.
(*She guides* MOLLY's *hand to the old man's, they touch. The children sneak looks at her, hide from her gaze, giggle.* SOLOMON *watches her for a moment, serious.*)
SOLOMON: Don't laugh at Molly. She is very strong, like her mother. Like we say, when you have touched the women, you have struck a rock. You have dislodged a boulder. You will be crushed.
(*MOLLY stares at him. Two of the women come out from the kitchen, carrying steaming plates, huge hunks of bread. They set them down in front of* ELSIE *and* MOLLY. SOLOMON *reaches across the table, puts something down in front of* MOLLY.)
I am giving this to you. (*The black, green and gold beaded bracelet.*)
MOLLY: Thank you.
SOLOMON: Let's eat.
(*MOLLY lifts her spoon, dips it into the bowl, stops. A chicken foot in the soup. She's shocked, looks up, looks across at* ELSIE.)
MOLLY: Elsie. There's a foot in my soup.
SOLOMON: It's the best part of the chicken. It will make you rich!
(*MOLLY looks at it.*)
MOLLY: (*Soft*) I can't.
(*She's absolutely panicked.* ELSIE *laughs, says something, reaches over to spoon out the foot, gives it to one of the children.*)

105. INT. TOWNSHIP CHURCH HALL. DAY
ELSIE *and* MOLLY *sit at the back facing a raised platform. The rows of benches packed with people, others stand.* HAROLD *to one side, his camera around his neck.*

SOLOMON *on the platform. A table covered with the black, green and yellow flag of the ANC. A banner, 'RELEASE OUR LEADERS'.*
*The African National Anthem. The harmonies deep and stirring, fists raised high in the air.* MOLLY *sings along, smiling with* ELSIE *because she knows the words. At the end, the ANC salute.*

SOLOMON: My mothers, my fathers, my brothers, my sisters – comrades all! I greet you in the name of the struggle.

ALL: *Amandla!*

SOLOMON: Thine Sizwe! We cry for our land! That's a cry each of us feels in his soul . . . a cry we hear in our sleep. These broken houses where we live, this poor church in which we meet, were not always here.
(*He looks at an old man.*)
You, Baba Masaleo –
(*He looks at an old woman.*)
You, *logo* Lusiti . . . you remember this place in another time when you were children –
(*Old man, old woman, nodding.*)
– a time when these slums were green fields and the land was ours. *Amandla!*

ALL: Ngawethu!

SOLOMON: And then the Dutchman came, and the Englishman came and planted their flags, and called our land theirs!

ALL: Thine Sizwe! Mayibuye!

SOLOMON: And in return, they filled our lives with such misery that for many years we forgot to dream of freedom. But fifty years ago we remembered, and our movement and our struggle began. We asked for a share of what was ours, and the dignity to live as fellow men. And when they did not hear us we raised our voices again and again. And what has been their reply? Taste the graveyards! They are salty with our people's blood!

ALL: Ubaba! Umama! Amandla!

SOLOMON: How long must we stand with our beggar's tins and cry Thine Sizwe! Thine Sizwe!! The time has come for a different cry! Forward with the armed struggle! Phambile namabutho ka Mandela! Phambile namabutho ka Lhutuli! Umkhonto We Sizwe!

106. EXT. TOWNSHIP CHURCH HALL. DAY
*A young boy bangs furiously on a gong suspended from a tree.*


107. EXT. TOWNSHIP STREET. DAY
*A police convoy, racing towards the hall.*


108. INT. TOWNSHIP CHURCH HALL. DAY
*Silence, as a white priest steps forward to take* SOLOMON's *place.*


109. EXT. TOWNSHIP CHURCH HALL. DAY
*Armed uniformed police, some with dogs, burst into the hall.*


110. INT. TOWNSHIP CHURCH HALL. DAY
*The 'congregation' are singing a hymn, 'Amazing Grace'. The police burst in, surround the hall. Two policemen, obviously in charge, march down the hall to the raised platform.*
POLICEMAN: We're taking you in. We know you.
> (*They drag* SOLOMON *from the hall, beating him as he resists. Others are arrested, beaten.* HAROLD *has his camera smashed, and is dragged out of the hall.*
> *On* MOLLY, *staring as they drag* SOLOMON *away, transfixed by the red blood on black skin.*
> *Gradually, and building to a crescendo, the women begin a wailing chant, deep and high in their throats.*)


111. INT. POLICE CAR. DAY
*Two policemen in the front,* ELSIE *and* MOLLY *at the back. The police radio on, static.*
MOLLY *looks down, fingering the bracelet in her lap. Then she looks at* ELSIE, *sees her averted face, the tears on her cheeks.*


112. INT. PRISON CORRIDORS. DAY
SOLOMON, *bruised, bleeding, pushed along the corridors. Two uniformed policemen hurl a continuous stream of abuse at him, in English and Afrikaans.*


113. INT. PRISON INTERROGATION ROOM. DAY
SOLOMON *is handcuffed to a chair. Prominent in the room is a large container filled with water. Canes in the container, upright,*

*bobbing about, expanding.*
*Close on* SOLOMON. *Naked fear.*

114. INT. DIANA'S STUDY. DAY
*Shuttered, dim.* MOLLY *locks the door, kneels by the side of the*
*desk, feeling for the hidden catch. Then suddenly she locates the*
*spring, is startled as the hidden door swings open.*
*Inside are typewritten lists, address books, notebooks, technical*
*diagrams, plans of industrial complexes. She closes the drawer.*

115. EXT. SUBURBAN GROCERY STORE. DAY
MOLLY *and* BERTHA *enter the store. Near by, a young African*
*Newsvendor. Headlines displayed: 'VICTIMS IN BOMB*
*BLAST'.*

116. INT. SUBURBAN GROCERY STORE. DAY
*A woman paying for her groceries at the counter. She turns around.*
*It's* JUNE, *caught off guard as she sees* BERTHA *and* MOLLY. *She*
*stammers a greeting.* BERTHA *ignores her, frosty.*
*At the door* JUNE *pauses, then turns back. She goes to* MOLLY,
*touches her awkwardly on the arm.*
JUNE: Honey, are you all right?
    (MOLLY *nods, threatening tears.*)
    Look . . . I'm sorry . . . Gerald . . . there are things he

86

doesn't agree with. That's why he . . . behaves like he
does.
(*A pause.*)
Look . . . I'm sorry . . .
(*She squeezes* MOLLY's *arm, turns, walks hurriedly out of the
store.*)

## 117. INT. PRISON CELL. NIGHT
DIANA, *asleep under the blanket, an arm shielding her face from the
burning light bulb.*
*The door opens. She starts awake, stares at the* WARDRESS.
WARDRESS: Get dressed. Hurry. They're waiting for you.

## 118. INT. PRISON INTERROGATION ROOM. NIGHT
MULLER *and* LE ROUX *are waiting.* LE ROUX *stands, looking
even more angry than usual.* MULLER *sits on the edge of the desk.*
DIANA, *hastily dressed, paler, thinner, led into the room. She stands
– there are no chairs in the room.*
DIANA: (*Flippant*) This is very dramatic.
    (LE ROUX, *coiled, thrusts a photograph at her. It shows,
    graphically, white victims of a bomb explosion.*
    DIANA *looks away immediately.* LE ROUX *holds up another
    photograph. She won't look. He thrusts it in her face.*)
LE ROUX: How would you feel if this was your family, your

husband, your children. . . ? This is what you people do. Murderers!

DIANA: *You* want to talk about murderers? Why don't you show me the pictures of the sixty-nine you murdered at Sharpeville –

(LE ROUX *hits her, hard. She's stunned for a moment, then in shock.*)

MULLER: (*In Afrikaans, to* LE ROUX) You better get out of here.

(LE ROUX *swears, leaves.* MULLER *watches* DIANA *for a moment. She's shaking.*)

Perhaps we can arrange for you to see your children.

### 119. INT. PRISON CORRIDOR. DAY

*The children follow* BERTHA *and a wardress down the corridor, past heavy doors and meshed and barred windows.* BERTHA *is carrying a food basket, covered with a white cloth.*

*From one of the open doorways the sound of intermittently shouted commands, then loud female laughter. The children stop, hang back, held by the sight.*

### 120. INT. PRISON ROOM, CHILDREN'S POV: DAY

*Under the watchful eyes of two wardresses, three African prisoners in ragged shirts and dirty singlets polish the bright red concrete floor. Each prisoner stands with one or both feet on a cleaning rag, and as the wardresses shriek 'twist', they propel the rags around the room, in a grotesque parody of the dance. The wardresses shriek with laughter.*

### 121. INT. PRISON CORRIDOR. DAY

BERTHA *pulls the children back in line and they continue along the corridor.*

### 122. INT. SECURITY BRANCH CAR, MOVING THROUGH CITY. DAY

DIANA, *in the back, in between two plainclothes policemen. Two others in the front.*

*The* POLICEMAN *in the passenger seat turns around to face* DIANA.

POLICEMAN: We're taking you on a goodbye tour.

(*The car slows down, then stops across the street from the*

*midtown apartment building in scene 21.* GEORGE, *the*
*caretaker, is cleaning the entrance.* DIANA *sees him, then*
*quickly turns away.*
*The car drives off.* GEORGE *stares after it.*)


### 123. EXT. PRISON YARD. DAY
*The* CHILDREN *and* BERTHA *sit in a circle. The food basket is on*
*the ground in the middle. A wardress stands in one corner.*
*Off screen the sound of approaching footsteps.* BERTHA *leans over to*
*adjust a ribbon in* MIRIAM's *hair. On* MOLLY, *tense, expectant.*
MULLER *comes into the courtyard.*
MULLER: She's been transferred, Mrs Abrahams. To Pretoria.
   (*On* BERTHA – *she can't believe what he says.* MOLLY *jumps*
   *out of her chair.*)
MOLLY: Then why did you make us come here?
MULLER: We tried to reach you . . .
MOLLY: When? When did you try to reach us? There's always
   someone at the house . . .
   (MULLER *turns to leave.*)
   What about the food . . .
   (*The children watch as* BERTHA *gets up. She seems totally*
   *disoriented, unable to focus.*)


### 124. INT. PRISON CORRIDOR. DAY
*The children watch as* BERTHA *strides stiffly down the corridor,*
*heels clacking on the concrete floor.*
MOLLY: (*Shouting after her*) What about the food?
   (BERTHA *doesn't look back.*)


### 125. INT. PRISON CELL, PRETORIA. DAY
*Newer, but smaller than the first. No window.*
DIANA *slowly unpicks the hem of her dress. She holds up the needle*
*to thread by the light.*


### 126. INT. ROTH DINING ROOM. DAY
ELSIE *serves tea to the children. They all look miserable, scared,*
*picking at their food.*
HAROLD *comes into the room.*
HAROLD: It's nothing serious. Your granny's just under a lot of

strain. She's going to go away to rest, for a few weeks.
You'll come and stay with us –
MOLLY: (*Quickly*) I want to stay here –
MIRIAM: – Me too –
MOLLY: Elsie will be here. I want to stay with her.
ELSIE: Molly. I have to be with my family. I won't be here.
(MOLLY *looks at her. She's devastated. Finally:*)
MOLLY: Then I want to go to the school. I want to be a
boarder.
MIRIAM: Molly, can I come with you . . .
(JUDE *walks out of the room.*)

## 127. INT. PRISON CELL, PRETORIA. DAY
DIANA *on the mat, reading the Bible.*
*The door opens. The wardress stands aside and* MULLER *walks in.*
DIANA *jumps up.*
DIANA: What do you want?
MULLER: I dropped by to see you.
DIANA: Where's your friend?
MULLER: Why, are you missing him?
DIANA: At least he's honest.
MULLER: And what do you think of me?
DIANA: I don't think about you at all.
MULLER: Would you prefer someone else to question you?
DIANA: It makes no earthly difference to me.
(*A pause. They stare at each other.*)
My ninety days is up in ten days' time. (*A pause.*) Are you
going to charge me? (*A pause.*) Tell me.
MULLER: I brought you something.
(*He hands her two books.*)

## 128. INT. DORMITORY. DAY
*It's very tidy, beds neatly made.* MOLLY *watches as* YVONNE *and*
DEBBIE *look around, curiously.*
YVONNE: I don't know . . . I think I like my own room better,
thank you very much.
DEBBIE: Don't you all have fun?
MOLLY: What do you mean?
DEBBIE: Pillow fights, midnight feasts . . .
YVONNE: Where does Whitworth sleep?

91

MOLLY: Next door.

YVONNE: (*Conspiratorial*) Let's apple-pie her bed!

DEBBIE: (*Excited*) Oh, fab. Quick! Come on, Molly . . .

    (*They walk to the door.*)

MOLLY: No. Don't.

    (*They stop, stare at her.*)

YVONNE: Oh, come on, Molly. She'll never know it was us.

MOLLY: No.

YVONNE: Why not? She's such a bitch.

    (MOLLY *silent.* YVONNE *looks at her.*)

DEBBIE: We better go.

    (*They walk away.* MOLLY *looks after them, miserable.*)

## 129. INT. PRISON INTERROGATION ROOM, PRETORIA. DAY

DIANA *with* MULLER. *She looks exhausted, thin, fraught.*

DIANA: I'm still in pain. I'm not sleeping. I'm out of sleeping
    pills.

MULLER: I'll speak to the doctor. But unless you start eating,
    they won't do you much good.

    (*A pause.*)

    Do you miss your children?

DIANA: Why do you ask?

MULLER: Why don't you answer?

DIANA: Because it's a stupid question.

    (*A pause.*)

MULLER: Molly's not so crazy about boarding school.

DIANA: Boarding school?

MULLER: And the little ones aren't crazy about staying at
    Harold's.

DIANA: What's going on? Where's my mother?

MULLER: She's taken a little trip –

DIANA: What do you mean? Where is she? Have you taken her
    in?

MULLER: Do you think you're the only person in this country
    that suffers the consequences of your politics?

DIANA: (*Very agitated*) You're wasting your time. I will make no
    statement because you're out to trap me!

MULLER: How can we trap you on your own statement if we
    don't have evidence?

DIANA: You'll make it up if you haven't got it!

MULLER: You've got a twisted mind!

DIANA: (*On her feet*) You follow me, open my letters, tap my telephone, arrest me . . . And now you want me to believe that you'll come to a free and unprejudiced decision on my future?!!! *I do not trust you.*

MULLER: *Then you have nothing left to trust!* Your people have denounced you publicly. One of your friends saw you in the Security Branch car. Someone's been naming names and they think it's you . . .

DIANA: (*Low*) You bastard . . .

MULLER: (*Continuing*) Your family is suffering because of your delusions. All this hand-wringing, and playing Joan of Arc is nothing but an excuse for being a terrible mother! (*He's screaming at her now.*) Unless you make a statement, you will die in your cell and *no one* will know what happened!! (*A pause.* DIANA *starts to laugh, hysterical.* MULLER *looks at her in disgust.*)
You've wasted your life. You might have done so much . . .
(*Her laughter dies.*)

130. INT. PRISON CORRIDOR, PRETORIA. DAY
DIANA *led by a* WARDRESS *along the corridor back to her cell.*

131. INT. CELL, PRETORIA. DAY
*The door is locked behind her. She walks over to the mat, stops, stares at it. She lifts the blanket, pulls the mat out from the wall. She searches frantically around the cell. Then she hammers with her fists against the door, kicking out at it.*

WARDRESS: (*Off screen*) And now what's the matter?

DIANA: Where are my books?

WARDRESS: (*Off screen*) Your books? You're not allowed to have books.
(DIANA *throws her possessions and the cell's contents around the cell, sobbing, screaming.*)

132. INT. PRISON CORRIDOR OUTSIDE CELL, PRETORIA. DAY
*The* WARDRESS *watches.*

93

133. EXT. SCHOOL SWIMMING POOL. DAY
MOLLY, *with other girls, lined up by the pool. Regulation swimsuits and caps. They're diving, one by one. An instructor watches them. A younger girl comes into the enclosure, hands a note to the instructor. She reads it, calls to* MOLLY, *says something to her. The other girls watch as she runs off,* YVONNE *among them.*

134. EXT. SCHOOL ENTRANCE. DAY
BERTHA, *waiting by her car.* MIRIAM *and* JUDE, *greeting her excitedly as* MOLLY, *in uniform, with wet hair, runs out.*
MOLLY, *shy with* BERTHA.
MOLLY: Are you better?
BERTHA: Much better, thank you, darling.
MOLLY: Where are we going?
BERTHA: To see Mommy.
   (MOLLY *stares at her.*)
MOLLY: I don't want to go, Gran. They'll do it again.

135. INT. PRISON VISITING ROOM, PRETORIA. DAY
*The children sit closely together, waiting in silence. A wardress to one side.*
*Off screen the sound of approaching footsteps. The door opens.*

DIANA, *flanked by* MULLER. *She's wearing lipstick, has tried to fix her hair.*
*The children run to her, jostle to reach her, hug her. She hugs them in turn.* MOLLY's *face clenched to hold back the tears.*
DIANA *embraces* BERTHA.
BERTHA: (*Whispering*) Are you cracking up?
   (DIANA *nods.*)
   We're depending on you.
   (DIANA *releases her, turns to* MULLER.)
DIANA: Can I be alone with my children?
MULLER: I won't say a word. Try and ignore me. Forget I'm here.
   (MIRIAM *tugs at* DIANA.)
MIRIAM: Mommy, Mommy . . . look what we brought you.
   (*She takes out a handful of bubble-gum from a pocket.* DIANA *is surprised.*)
DIANA: Thank you, darling. Bubble-gum.
   (MIRIAM *leans over to hiss in her hair.*)
MIRIAM: Open one. Open one and then you'll see.
   (DIANA *unwraps one.*)
DIANA: (*Reading from the wrapper*) 'Did you know that the skin of an elephant is one inch thick? Did you know that zip fasteners were first used in the nineteenth century? . . .'
MIRIAM: (*Loud whisper*) See? It's something for you to read . . .
DIANA: (*Laughing*) Thank you, darling.
   (MOLLY *can't stop staring at her mother, taking in her white legs, how thin she is, her lank hair. She looks at* MULLER, *he smiles at her. She turns quickly away.*)
   Molly. Darling, how's school? How is Yvonne?
   (MOLLY *looks down.*)
MOLLY: We're not really friends any more.
MIRIAM: Gerald grabbed her and dragged her through the street . . .
MOLLY: (*Emphatic*) It doesn't matter any more.
   (DIANA *looks at her, helpless.*)
DIANA: I know. It's hard. But you'll make new friends.
   (MOLLY *starts to cry, silent tears running down her face.*
   DIANA *puts* MIRIAM *down, gets up, goes over to her, hugs her in her chair.*)
MOLLY: (*Sobbing*) It's horrible. I hate the school. And I don't

know what's going to happen . . .
(DIANA *holds her, fighting to keep back her own tears.*
MIRIAM *and* JUDE *look weary.* MULLER, *watching,*
*impassive.*)
DIANA: (*Whispering*) Don't, darling. Don't cry here. Not here.
Not in front of them . . .

136. EXT. STREET OUTSIDE THE PRISON. DAY
*Bertha's car emerges from the prison into the street.*
*Across the street from the prison a large group are gathered, black*
*and white, many women. They hold placards and posters denouncing*
*the regime and demanding the release of political detainees, among*
*them Diana Roth.*
*Near by are police with dogs. The demonstrators start to sing.*

137. INT. BERTHA'S CAR. DAY
MOLLY's *face pressed against the window.*

138. INT. SCHOOL DORMITORY. DAWN
MOLLY *wide awake. The other girls asleep. She's holding the*
*notebook, a pen in her hand. Insert: the notebook, the pen resting at*
*the number 89, heavily circled.* MOLLY *starts counting again from*
*the first mark, rhythmically, in twos.*

139. INT. PRISON CELL, PRETORIA. DAY
DIANA *is hemming slowly, precisely. The door opens. A*
WARDRESS, *with a* PRISON OFFICER.
PRISON OFFICER: Pack your things, Mrs Roth. We're releasing
you.
(DIANA *stares at him, not moving.*)
Come on. We're releasing you.
DIANA: Let me see the release order.
PRISON OFFICER: The duty sergeant has it.
(DIANA *doesn't move.*)
WARDRESS: Come on, don't be like that. Here's your chance to
.go home. Come, I'll help you pack.

140. INT. PRISON OFFICE. DAY
DIANA *stands in front of the* DUTY SERGEANT, *her suitcase on the*
*floor next to her. He hands her a form.*

DUTY SERGEANT: Your release papers.

DIANA: Can I use the phone?

DUTY SERGEANT: There's a public phone on the street outside.
You can leave your suitcase here.

DIANA: I'll take it with me.
(*She walks to the door, then stops. She drops the suitcase and
goes back to the* DUTY SERGEANT. *He stares at her.*)
I haven't got any money.

141. EXT. STREET OUTSIDE THE PRISON. DAY

DIANA *blinks in the sunshine. She walks quickly over to the
telephone kiosk, picks up the phone, starts to dial.
The door opens.* TWO POLICEMEN, *in plain clothes, stand outside.*

FIRST MAN: Diana Roth?
(*She looks at them.*)
We're arresting you. Clause seventeen of the General Law
Amendment Act of 1963. Ninety days.

142. INT. PRISON CORRIDOR, PRETORIA. DAY

DIANA, *accompanied by two wardresses, led down the corridor, back
to the cell. Tears pouring down her face.*

143. EXT. SCHOOL ENTRANCE. DAY

MOLLY *walks slowly to where* HAROLD *sits waiting, in his parked
car.*

HAROLD: Are you OK?
(*She nods.*)
Come and sit in here.
(*She shakes her head.* HAROLD *looks at her, gets out of the
car. A few girls, passing by in the background, stare, curious.*)
(*Slow, awkward*) I haven't spoken to your sisters but
you're old enough – and you understand – I think you do
. . . You must try and prepare yourself so that you're not
disappointed . . . It's very good news that they haven't
charged her, but they could keep her in prison for a long
time . . .

MOLLY: (*A whisper*) But we're by ourselves . . . (*In spite of
herself, she's crying.*)

HAROLD: Elsie's children have been on their own all their lives.

MOLLY: I know. But I'm not talking about them.

HAROLD: But you always have to. (*A pause.*) How can you live here and do nothing?

MOLLY: Lots of people do.

HAROLD: And what do you think of them?

(*She doesn't answer.*)

We also have to live with ourselves. Not just for now but for later as well. (*A pause. Gentle*) Do you understand?

(*A pause.*)

MOLLY: Sometimes I do. Sometimes I don't. What's the difference?


144. INT. PRISON INTERROGATION ROOM, PRETORIA. DAY

DIANA, *haggard, no make-up for the first time. Besides* MULLER *and* LE ROUX, *there are three plain clothes policemen in the room. It's been a long session.*

LE ROUX: Who did you see most at these meetings?

DIANA: Adrian Lee, Petrus Nkosi, Yusaf Patel . . .

LE ROUX: Where did these meetings take place?

DIANA: In my house, in my motor car, in the home of Ivan Stanley.

(*A pause.* MULLER *stares across at her.*)

MULLER: (*Ice cold*) It's a funny thing, isn't it? Every name you've given us is the name of someone who's left the country. (*He screws up a piece of paper.*) We know every meeting you attended – we saw you come, we saw you go – and you were the only woman there. And you pretend that you know nothing of what happened – that nothing happened worth knowing. We have enough evidence to charge you over and over again, right here and now. But we happen to have respect for women in this country, and we're going to give you one more chance. (*A pause.*) We'll continue tomorrow.

(*He stands, gathers together the things on the desk. The other men put on their jackets. One of them moves to stand in front of* DIANA.)

POLICEMAN: (*Soft, measured*) We've dealt with you Communists before. And we've learnt that you have to be put against the wall and squeezed, pushed and squeezed and squashed into a corner. Then you

change. Then you talk. (*To* MULLER) She's too
comfortable here. We should move her downstairs.
(*He walks out of the room, followed by the others. Only*
MULLER *remains.* DIANA *shaken, trembling.*)
DIANA: I will not make another statement.
(MULLER *stares at her.*)
MULLER: I'm sorry. I'm truly sorry that you're doing this to
yourself. I don't know whether I'll be seeing you any more
. . . What can I say? (*He shrugs.*) Good luck.


145. INT. PRISON CELL, PRETORIA. NIGHT
DIANA *writes on the inside covers of the Bible with a stub of
eyebrow pencil.*
DIANA: (*Reading aloud, soft*) 'This is a strange place for this
message . . .'
(*The door opens. She closes the book. The* WARDRESS *comes
in, takes the untouched tray from the chair.*)
WARDRESS: You really should eat, you know. It doesn't make
sense – you're the one who's going to suffer.
(*She leaves.* DIANA *listens to her retreating footsteps then gets
up, fills a glass with water, takes out a handful of hoarded pills
from the lining of her suitcase.*)


146. INT. PRISON CORRIDORS, PRETORIA. NIGHT
*A frightened-looking* WARDRESS *leads* MULLER *quickly down the
corridors. He looks furious.*
*She unlocks an outer gate. The door to Diana's cell is wide
open.*
MULLER *stops at the door, then steps back and aside to let a doctor
and two orderlies pass. They are carrying* DIANA *on a stretcher. Her
eyes are closed.* MULLER *follows them.*


147. INT. HOSPITAL ROOM. DAY
DIANA *lies in bed attached to a drip, expressionless.* MULLER *comes
into the room. She looks away.*
MULLER: That wasn't very clever. Or maybe it was . . . We're
releasing you. But we're placing you under twenty-four-
hour house arrest. Any visitors will have to get our
permission first. And anyone who publishes your writing,
or quotes you either directly or indirectly

will be in violation of the law. (*A pause.*) You're lucky
we found you in time. (*He smiles.*) Did you think we
wouldn't?
(DIANA, *expressionless.* MULLER *turns and walks away.*)

148. INT. ROTH HOUSE. DAY
MOLLY, *in school uniform and hat, racing through the house,
searching. Then she runs down the corridor to Diana's room.*

149. INT. DIANA'S ROOM. DAY
*She bursts in, stops. The room is dim, the curtains pulled to.*
DIANA *is in bed. She looks very weak.* BERTHA *sits at the side,*
MIRIAM *and* JUDE *on the bed.* MOLLY *stares at her mother.*
DIANA *holds out her arms, smiling.* MOLLY *hugs her tightly.
After a moment,* DIANA *gently disengages herself.* MOLLY
*stands at the side of the bed. She can't stop staring at her
mother.*
MOLLY: What's wrong with you? What did they do?
DIANA: I know, I look a bit scary. I'm just very tired,
    darling. I've been sick.
MIRIAM: Mom was in an ambulance.
MOLLY: Did they torture you?

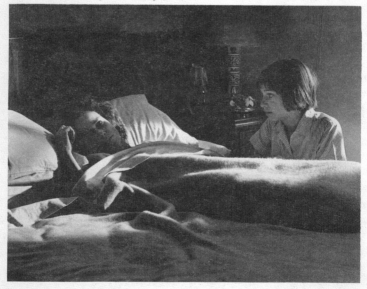

(DIANA *looks away.*)

BERTHA: Don't ask all these questions. Your mother's
tired –

MOLLY: They torture Solomon. Elsie says they put wires all
over his body and then give him electric shocks . . .
(*She stops.* DIANA *turns her face to the wall.* JUDE *moves
nearer to her to hug her.* MOLLY *looks distraught.*)

BERTHA: Come on. Let's leave Mom to sleep.
(*She ushers them out of the room.* MOLLY *turns at the
doorway.*)

MOLLY: Shall I bring you a cup of tea?

DIANA: No. Come back later.


150. INT. KITCHEN. DAY
*The children at tea around the kitchen table. They're
unnaturally quiet, subdued, polite, picking at the food.* BERTHA
*to one side, baking, getting in* MILIUS'S *way.* MOLLY *watches
as he places a single flower on the tea tray he's preparing.*

MOLLY: Milius, let me take it to her. Please. I'll tell her the
flowers came from you.

MIRIAM: Me too. I'll help you, Molly –

BERTHA: No, Miriam. Let her go alone.
(MOLLY *looks at* BERTHA *in surprise, lifts the tray.*)


151. INT. DIANA'S ROOM. DAY
MOLLY *comes in backwards, balancing the tray.* DIANA
*suddenly wakes, sits bolt upright, screams.* MOLLY, *startled,
drops the tray. There's a resounding crash.*

MOLLY: I dropped the tray. Sorry. I dropped the tray.
(MILIUS *comes rushing into the room.* BERTHA,
*breathless, pushes past him.* DIANA *is shaking, her head in
her hands.*)
I dropped the tray.

BERTHA: Diana, I'm going to call the doctor –

DIANA: No. I'll be OK.
(MILIUS *starts to clear up the mess.* MOLLY *hovers, then,
on the verge of tears, walks out of the room.*)


152. EXT. STREET OUTSIDE ROTH HOUSE. DAY
*An unmarked police car parked across the street. Two*

*plainclothes policemen keeping watch on the house. They're*
*smiling. What they see:* MOLLY, *swinging on the gate, staring*
*at them. She looks down the street. What she sees: in the*
*distance, approaching the house, two African men. One is*
*Solomon's and Elsie's cousin.* MOLLY *runs down the street to*
*them. Words pass between them, then she turns and races back*
*into the house.*

153. EXT. ROTH KITCHEN. DAY
ELSIE, *at work in the kitchen.* MIRIAM *at the table, drawing.*
MOLLY: Your cousin's here. Something's happened.
   (ELSIE *stares at her for a moment, then runs out of the*
   *kitchen.*)

153. INT. DIANA'S BEDROOM. DAY
DIANA, *resting on the bed. She looks a little stronger, less pale.*
MOLLY *bursts into the room.*
MOLLY: Mom. You better come. Something's happened.

155. EXT. STREET OUTSIDE ROTH HOUSE. DAY
ELSIE *with the two African men, her back to us. One of the*
*men is talking to her, his hand on her arm. She stands stock still*
*for a moment. Then she turns, breaks away from the man's hold*
*on her, staggers wildly along the street.*

ELSIE: (*Screaming*) Solomon. Solomon. They killed him.
(*A powerful mix of anger and grief.*
DIANA *comes running from the house.* MOLLY, JUDE *and*
MIRIAM *with her.* MILIUS *comes running from the*
*garden. As* DIANA *runs towards* ELSIE, *the policemen get*
*out of the car, hesitate, unsure.*
ELSIE *pushes past* DIANA, *distraught, weeping.*)
They killed him.
(*They follow her into the house.* MOLLY *stares at the*
*policemen, then marches across the road, right up to them.*)
MOLLY: (*Screaming*) Why don't you go away and leave us
alone!


156. INT. MOLLY'S ROOM. NIGHT
MOLLY *lies awake. She lifts her arm, stares at Solomon's*
*bracelet around her wrist in the moonlight.*

157. INT. DIANA'S STUDY. NIGHT
MOLLY *bends down by the side of the desk. She feels with her*
*fingers for the hidden catch. The panel swings out. There's*
*nothing in the hidden compartment but the Bible from the*
*prison. She opens it to the fly-leaf pages. Diana's handwriting.*
*She reads part of it aloud.*
MOLLY: 'My Gus . . . this is a strange place for this
message, but it's the only way I can say goodbye. We
never planned for these times, did we . . . I can't
imagine life outside of here . . . I apologize for my
cowardice . . . I have not given in . . . I love you all so
much . . .' (*She stands for a moment, stock still. Then she*
*closes the Bible and puts it back down on the desk.*)

158. INT. ROTH DINING ROOM. DAY
*The family sits around a loaded birthday table.* MIRIAM *is at*
*the head, unwrapping presents.* DIANA *is with them, dressed,*
*made-up, still a little pale.* MOLLY *seems subdued. They're all*
*wearing party hats.* MIRIAM *unwraps a large doll. She's*
*thrilled with it. Then she looks at* DIANA.
MIRIAM: But how did you get it? You can't go out to the
shops.
(DIANA *smiles at her.*)

DIANA: Magic.
(MILIUS *comes out from the kitchen, carrying a birthday cake, candles alight. He holds it in front of* MIRIAM. *She takes a deep breath, blows out the candles.*)
ALL:

> Happy Birthday to you
> Happy Birthday to you
> Happy Birthday dear Miriam . . .

(*There's a hammering at the door.* DIANA *jumps.* MILIUS *leaves the room.*
DIANA *gets up, pulling off her party hat. She's shaking.*
MOLLY *looks terrified.*
MILIUS *comes back into the room with* KRUGER *and two uniformed policemen.*)
KRUGER: We're just checking, Mrs Roth.
DIANA: You keep a twenty-four-hour watch on this house. How could I leave?
KRUGER: We're going to take a look around.
(*They walk through to the sitting room.* MOLLY *gets up from the table.*)
DIANA: Molly. Stay here.
(MOLLY *ignores her, walks out of the room.*)

159. INT. DIANA'S STUDY. DAY
MOLLY *stands in the doorway.* KRUGER *is at the window, staring out at the garden.*
*An over-zealous policeman is examining the desk. He opens the drawers, peers along the sides and underneath.*
DIANA *appears at the doorway, behind* MOLLY.
*The policeman slides the drawers in and out, peering in, tapping the wood on the outside.*
MOLLY *watches him, then looks at* KRUGER, *who is examining items on the desk. He picks up the Bible. Smiles.* MOLLY *takes a deep breath, runs across the room, throws herself at him, pushing him with all her strength.*
KRUGER: She's mad! She's crazy!
(*He moves towards her.* DIANA *comes forward.*)
DIANA: She's a child!
KRUGER: She's not a child. She's an animal.

106

(DIANA *places herself between him and* MOLLY.
BERTHA, JUDE *and* MIRIAM *behind her, in the doorway.*
DIANA, *tall with fury.*)

DIANA: (*Softly*) Get out of my house.

KRUGER: Be careful what you say, Mrs Roth –
(DIANA *stares at him, unwavering.*)

DIANA: I'm not going to say any more. Get out of my house.
(KRUGER *stares at her for a moment, then motions to his
men to follow him.*
DIANA *slams the door behind them. She turns on* MOLLY,
*furious.*)
Can't you understand? You mustn't let them see how
they affect you. It only makes it worse.

MOLLY: Why are you angry with *me*? After what you tried
to do.

DIANA: What did I do?

MOLLY: You know . . .

DIANA: (*Shouting*) No. I don't know. What did I do?

MOLLY: (*Screaming*) You tried to kill yourself. I read what
you wrote.
(DIANA, *stunned for a moment.*)

DIANA: You should be ashamed of yourself. I told you not
to look in that drawer. I trusted you. That was a secret
place, I asked you to respect that –

MOLLY: Stop talking about that stupid drawer.
(*She looks at her mother, full in the face.* DIANA *stares
back at her, shaken.*)
You tried to leave us. You don't care about us. You
shouldn't have had us.
(*She tries to walk out of the room.* DIANA *grabs her, holds
on to her.* MOLLY *stiff and unyielding.*)

DIANA: Stay here. We have to talk –

MOLLY: I don't want to stay with you. I don't want to talk
to you –

DIANA: Well, I want to talk to *you* . . .
(*Holding on to* MOLLY, *forcing her to listen.*)
Listen to me . . . I was breaking apart . . . what good
would I have been to you in pieces . . . I was afraid I
would have put other people in danger . . .

MOLLY: (*Bitter*) What people?

DIANA: Our friends, people like Harold –

MOLLY: *Your* friends. Your friends, your work, that's what's most important. That's all you care about.
(*A pause.*)

DIANA: All right. My friends. My work. But what we care about is the whole country.
(MOLLY *stares at her.*)

MOLLY: What about me?
(DIANA *stares at her.*)

DIANA: The whole country means you too. You live here, you eat here, I'm down the passage. But what about Elsie's children –

MOLLY: (*Interrupting*) I'm not Elsie's child. I'm your child –

DIANA: Listen to me! Elsie can't live with her children. Why? Because she's black. At Sharpeville people were shot down – shot in the back, shot running away – you've seen those pictures! Why? Because they were black. Solomon has been murdered. Why? Because he was black.

MOLLY: Stop treating me like a child. I know that!

DIANA: All right. I'm sorry. I know you do. But I also know how much you understand if you let yourself.

MOLLY: I never know what's going on. You never tell me anything . . .

DIANA: We can't even talk amongst ourselves. It's not safe . . .

MOLLY: I don't even know where Daddy is . . . why he left . . . (*Crying*) It's not fair. You're never here for me. It's not fair . . .
(DIANA *reaches for her, takes her in her arms, holds her. Silence for a moment.*)

DIANA: You're right. It's not fair. It's not fair . . . and I'm so sorry it's not fair . . . (*A pause.*) You deserve to have a mother. Well, you do have one. Just not the way you want her. (*A pause.*) Would you have preferred it if we'd been different?

MOLLY: No. Yes.
(*She bursts into tears again.* DIANA *rocks her.*)

DIANA: (*Comfortingly, rhythmically*) Sssh . . . sssh . . . ssssh . . .

Molly, we love you. Me, Dad, we love you . . . (*A pause.*)
*I'm* not even sure where Daddy is . . . He's doing the work
that people like Nelson Mandela and Walter Sisulu should
be doing. If he hadn't left when he did, he would be with
them right now, serving a life sentence . . . Molly, times
have changed . . . The work has changed . . .
(*A pause.* DIANA *wipes* MOLLY's *tears.*)
Solomon's being buried tomorrow. I'm going to the
funeral.
MOLLY: But you can't leave the house. They'll arrest you again.
DIANA: Perhaps.
(*A pause.*)
MOLLY: Are you scared?
(*A pause.*)
DIANA: Yes. But Solomon was my friend.
MOLLY: I want to go.
(DIANA *looks at her.*)
DIANA: Are you sure?
MOLLY: He was my friend.

160. INT. TOWNSHIP CHURCH. DAY
*Close on Solomon's coffin.*
*The church is packed to overflowing. The choir leads the singing,*
*'Zithulele Mama', words of triumph and hope.*
MOURNERS:

| | |
|---|---|
| Zithulele Mama | Don't cry Mama |
| Noma sengifele lona | Even if I am dead |
| Izwe lakithi | I have died for my land |
| Izwe le South Africa | Our land, South Africa |
| Ngizobashiya mina | I will leave my people |
| Ngizobashiya abazali | I will leave my parents |
| Ngiye Kwamanya amazwe | I will go to other countries |
| Ngiyobe ngilwela lona | To fight for my land |
| Izwe lakithi | I will die for my land |
| Izwe le South Africa | Our land, South Africa. |

(*In the forefront of the congregation,* ELSIE, MILIUS,
THANDILE, *hers and Solomon's children. Near by:* DIANA,
BERTHA, MOLLY, HAROLD. *Other whites, various ages,*
*including priests, nuns, journalists.*

## 161. EXT. TOWNSHIP CHURCH. DAY

*The street filled with men, women, children. From inside the church, the sound of the song. Then the coffin, draped with the flag of the ANC, is carried out by pallbearers. At the front, the black youth Molly met at Solomon's house.*

*Led by the* PRIEST, *the mourners file out of the church, singing. Dotted about are posters of Solomon, held high in the air. A banner proclaims: 'KILL APARTHEID, NOT DETAINEES'; another: 'MANDELA, LEADER OF THE PEOPLE'.*

*Uniformed police patrols, black and white, in evidence on the edges of the route.*

*The procession moves down the street towards the cemetery.*

## 162. EXT. EDGES OF TOWNSHIP. DAY

*A police convoy and the armoured carriers of the military, approaching. A reconnaissance helicopter hovers above.*

## 163. EXT. CEMETERY. DAY

*Packed with mourners. Solomon's family,* DIANA, HAROLD *and* MOLLY *stand with the priest around the open grave.*

PRIEST: Solomon Mabusa was one of us. What he suffered, we all suffer. When he spoke out against injustice, he spoke as if from our mouths, with our words, with our longing for justice, with our strength. We do not mourn him, we honour him, and we say that the only true tribute to him is to pick up the spear from where it has fallen. His death will not bring an end to the struggle. It will only give it more life!

*(The crowd shouts its approval.)*

Solomon Mabusa is just one man. And when we defy them –

(*He looks directly at* DIANA.)
– when we resist in ourselves, when we resist in our
hundreds, when we resist in our thousands, in our millions,
then victory is certain. *Amandla!*
CROWD: *Ngawethu!*
(*The* PRIEST *leads them in the singing of the African national
anthem. Joyful and defiant.*
MOLLY *watches* DIANA *sing, her fist in the air. Then* MOLLY
*raises her own arm, sings with her.* DIANA *puts an arm around
her daughter.*
*At the edge of the cemetery, a breakaway crowd advancing on
the gathering security forces. Police firing tear gas. The
helicopter hovers lower.*
*The crowd undeterred. To one side, a boy bends to pick up a
rock, hurls it at the security forces.*
*Freeze frame.*